"But that's the same old idea," she grumbled.

"No, it ain't. Not our own dump. We ain't done Sarsaparilla since Christmas."

She began to grumble her way across the yard and into the house. A smell of sink strayed out of grey, unpainted weatherboard, to oppose the stench of crushed boggabri and cotton pear. Perhaps because Whalleys were in the bits-and-pieces trade their home was threatening to give in to them.

Wal Whalley did the dumps. Of course there were the other lurks besides. But no one had an eye like Wal for the things a person needs: dead batteries and musical bedsteads, a carpet you wouldn't notice was stained, wire, and again wire, clocks only waiting to jump back into the race of time. Objects of commerce and mystery littered Whalleys' back yard. Best of all, a rusty boiler into which the twins would climb to play at cubby.

"Eh? Waddaboutut?" Wal shouted, and pushed against his wife with his side.

She almost put her foot through the hole that had come in the kitchen boards.

2 **ain't:** *isn't; haven't.*
to do s.th. (coll.): hier: in etwas vorbeischauen.
2 f. **Sarsaparilla:** wie Barranugli fiktiver Vorort von Sydney, der als Schauplatz in Whites Werk wiederkehrt.
6 **weatherboard:** Verschalung.
stench: Geruch, Gestank.
6 f. **boggabri / cotton pear:** vermutl. Namen australischer Pflanzen.
8 **bits-and-pieces** (pl.): Krimskrams.
8 f. **to give in to s.o.:** jdm. nachgeben, sich jdm. ergeben.
11 **lurk** (Austral., slang): Job.
13 **bedstead:** Bettgestell.
17 **cubby** (coll.): Höhle, Kuschelecke, Kabuff.
18 **Waddaboutut?:** *What about it?*

"Waddabout what?"
Half-suspecting, she half-sniggered. Because Wal knew how to play on her weakness.
"The fuckun *idea*!"
So that she began again to grumble. As she slopped through the house her clothes irritated her skin. The sunlight fell yellow on the grey masses of the unmade beds, turned the fluff in the corners of the rooms to gold. Something was nagging at her, something heavy continued to weigh her down.
Of course. It was the funeral.
"Why, Wal," she said, the way she would suddenly come round, "you could certainly of thought of a worse idea. It'll keep the kids out of mischief. Wonder if that bloody Lummy's gunna decide to honour us?"
"One day I'll knock 'is block off," said Wal.
"He's only at the awkward age."
She stood at the window, looking as though she might know the hell of a lot. It was the funeral made her feel solemn. Brought the goose-flesh out on her.

2 **to half-snigger:** halb kichern.
3 **to play on s.th.:** sich etwas zunutze machen, auf etwas spekulieren.
4 **fuckun:** *fucking* (vulg.): beschissen.
5 **to slop** (coll.): (durch Schmutz) waten.
8 **fluff:** Staubflocke.
9 **to nag:** (fig.) nagen, bohren.
10 **to weigh s.o. down:** jdn. be-, niederdrücken.
12 f. **to come round** (fig.): einlenken.
13 **of thought:** *have thought.*
15 **gunna:** *going.*
16 **block** (slang): ‚Rübe'.
17 **awkward age:** schwieriges Alter.
19 **the hell of a lot** (coll.): eine verdammte Menge.
the funeral made: *the funeral which made.*
20 **goose-flesh:** Gänsehaut.

"Good job you thought about the dump," she said, outstaring a red-brick propriety the other side of the road. "If there's anythun gets me down, it's havin' ter watch a funeral pass."

"Won't be from 'ere," he consoled. "They took 'er away same evenun. It's gunna start from Jackson's Personal Service."

"Good job she popped off at the beginnun of the week. They're not so personal at the week-end."

She began to prepare for the journey to the dump. Pulled her frock down a bit. Slipped on a pair of shoes.

"Bet *She*'ll be relieved. Wouldn't show it, though. Not about 'er sister. I bet Daise stuck in 'er fuckun guts."

Then Mrs Whalley was compelled to return to the window. As if her instinct. And sure enough there She was. Looking inside the letter-box, as if she hadn't collected already. Bent above the brick pillar in which the letter-box had been cemented, Mrs Hogben's face wore all that people expect of the bereaved.

"Daise was all right," said Wal.

"Daise was all right," agreed his wife.

Suddenly she wondered: What if Wal, if Wal had ever . . .?

Mrs Whalley settled her hair. If she hadn't been all that

1 **good job** (coll.): nur gut, daß . . .
1 f. **to outstare:** mit Blicken bezwingen.
8 **to pop off** (coll.): ‚abkratzen'.
14 f. **to stick in s.o.'s guts** (slang): jdm. im Magen liegen (*guts* [pl.]: Inneres, Magen).
22 **the bereaved:** die Hinterbliebenen.

satisfied at home – and she *was* satisfied, her recollective eyes would admit – she too might have done a line like Daise Morrow.

Over the road Mrs Hogben was calling.

"Meg?" she called. "Marg*ret?*"

Though from pure habit, without direction. Her voice sounded thinner today.

Then Mrs Hogben went away.

"Once I got took to a funeral," Mrs Whalley said. "They made me look in the coffun. It was the bloke's wife. He was that cut up."

"Did yer have a squint?"

"Pretended to."

Wal Whalley was breathing hard in the airless room.

"How soon do yer reckon they begin ter smell?"

"Smell? They wouldn't let 'em!" his wife said very definite. "You're the one that smells, Wal. I wonder you don't think of takin' a bath."

But she liked his smell, for all that. It followed her out of the shadow into the strong shaft of light. Looking at each other their two bodies asserted themselves. Their faces were lit by the certainty of life.

Wal tweaked her left nipple.

1 **recollective:** erinnerungsvoll.
2 **to do a line:** sich auf einem Gebiet betätigen.
10 **bloke** (coll.): Kerl.
11 **to be cut up:** tief betrübt, schwer mitgenommen sein.
12 **to have a squint** (coll.): einen raschen Blick werfen.
19 **for all that:** trotz alledem.
20 **shaft:** Strahl.
23 **to tweak:** zwicken, kneifen.
nipple: Brustwarze.

"We'll slip inter the Bull on the way, and pick up those cold bottles."
He spoke soft for him.

Mrs Hogben called another once or twice. Inside the brick entrance the cool of the house struck at her. She liked it cool, but not cold, and this was if not exactly cold, anyway, too sudden. So now she whimpered, very faintly, for everything you have to suffer, and death on top of all. Although it was her sister Daise who had died, Mrs Hogben was crying for the death which was waiting to carry her off in turn. She called: "Me-ehg?" But no one ever came to your rescue. She stopped to loosen the soil round the roots of the aluminium plant. She always had to be doing something. It made her feel better.
Meg did not hear, of course. She was standing amongst the fuchsia bushes, looking out from their greenish shade. She was thin and freckly. She looked awful, because Mum had made her wear her uniform, because it was sort of a formal occasion, to Auntie Daise's funeral. In the circumstances she not only looked, but was thin. That Mrs Ireland who was all for sport had told her she must turn her toes out, and watch out – she might grow up knock-kneed besides.
So Meg Hogben was, and felt, altogether awful. Her skin was green, except when the war between light and

1 **to slip into s.th.** (coll.): mal bei, in etwas vorbeischauen.
3 **for him:** für jdn. wie ihn.
7 **to whimper:** wimmern.
13 **aluminium plant:** vermutl. Bezeichnung einer australischen Pflanze.
17 **freckly** (auch: *freckled*): sommersprossig.
23 **knock-kneed:** X-beinig.

shade worried her face into scraps, and the fuchsia tassels, trembling against her unknowing cheek, infused something of their own blood, brindled her with shifting crimson. Only her eyes resisted. They were not exactly an ordinary grey. Lorrae Jensen, who was blue, said they were the eyes of a mopey cat.

A bunch of six or seven kids from second-grade, Lorrae, Edna, Val, Sherry, Sue Smith, and Sue Goldstein, stuck together in the holidays, though Meg sometimes wondered why. The others had come around to Hogben's Tuesday evening.

Lorrae said: "We're going down to Barranugli pool Thursday. There's some boys Sherry knows with a couple of Gs. They've promised to take us for a run after we come out."

Meg did not know whether she was glad or ashamed.

"I can't," she said. "My auntie's died."

"Arrr!" their voices trailed.

They couldn't get away too quick, as if it had been something contagious.

But murmuring.

Meg sensed she had become temporarily important.

So now she was alone with her dead importance, in the fuchsia bushes, on the day of Auntie Daise's funeral.

1 f. **tassel:** (quastenförmige) Blütenstaude.
2 **to infuse:** einflößen, übertragen.
3 **to brindle:** sprenkeln.
6 **mopey:** trübselig.
7 **bunch** (coll.): Haufen, Horde.
14 **G:** vermutl. etwa: Feuerstuhl.
to take s.o. for a run: jdn. auf eine Spritztour mitnehmen.
18 **arr:** Ausruf; etwa: och, ach.
to trail: verhallen, gedehnt klingen.
20 **contagious:** ansteckend.

She had turned fourteen. She remembered the ring in plaited gold Auntie Daise had promised her. When I am gone, her aunt had said. And now it had really happened. Without rancour Meg suspected there hadn't been time to think about the ring, and Mum would grab it, to add to all the other things she had.
Then that Lummy Whalley showed up, amongst the camphor laurels opposite, tossing his head of bleached hair. She hated boys with white hair. For that matter she hated boys, or any intrusion on her privacy. She hated Lum most of all. The day he threw the dog poo at her. It made the gristle come in her neck. Ugh! Although the old poo had only skittered over her skin, too dry to really matter, she had gone in and cried because, well, there were times when she cultivated dignity.
Now Meg Hogben and Lummy Whalley did not notice each other even when they looked.

"Who wants Meg Skinny-leg?
I'd rather take the clothes-peg . . ."

2 **to plait:** flechten.
4 **rancour:** Groll.
5 **mum:** Mami.
to grab: (gierig) schnappen, einheimsen.
8 **camphor laurel:** Kampferbaum (Lorbeergewächs).
to bleach: bleichen.
10 **intrusion:** Eindringen, Störung.
11 **poo** (coll.): Aa.
12 **to make the gristle come in s.o.'s neck:** etwa: jdm. den Hals zuschnüren (*gristle:* Knorpel).
ugh!: ih!
13 **to skitter:** entlangstreifen.
18 **Skinny-leg:** sprechender Name; etwa: Magerbein.
19 **clothes-peg:** Wäscheklammer (typischer Reim im nonsensartigen Kindervers).

Lum Whalley vibrated like a comb-and-paper over amongst the camphor laurels they lopped back every so many years for firewood. He slashed with his knife into bark. Once in a hot dusk he had carved I LOVE MEG, because that was something you did, like on lavatory walls, and in the trains, but it didn't mean anything of course. Afterwards he slashed the darkness as if it had been a train seat.

Lum Whalley pretended not to watch Meg Hogben skulking in the fuchsia bushes. Wearing her brown uniform. Stiffer, browner than for school, because it was her auntie's funeral.

"Me-ehg?" called Mrs Hogben. "Meg!"

"Lummy! Where the devil are yer?" called his mum. She was calling all around, in the woodshed, behind the dunny. Let her!

"Lum? Lummy, for Chris*sake*!" she called.

He hated that. Like some bloody kid. At school he had got them to call him Bill, halfway between, not so shameful as Lum, nor yet as awful as William.

Mrs Whalley came round the corner.

"Shoutin' me bloody lungs up!" she said. "When your dad's got a nice idea. We're goin' down to Sarsaparilla dump."

"Arr!" he said.

2 **to lop back:** (Baum, Hecke) zurückstutzen, -schneiden.
2 f. **every so many years:** alle paar Jahre.
3 **to slash:** (drauf)losstechen, aufschlitzen.
5 **lavatory:** Toilette.
10 **to skulk:** sich drücken, verkriechen; lauern.
16 **dunny** (Austral., slang): Plumpsklo.
17 **for Chrissake** (slang): *for Christ's sake:* um Himmels willen.
22 **me:** *my.*

But didn't spit.

"What gets inter you?" she asked.

Even at their most inaccessible Mrs Whalley liked to finger her children. Touch often assisted thought. But she liked the feel of them as well. She was glad she hadn't had girls. Boys turned into men, and you couldn't do without men, even when they took you for a mug, or got shickered, or bashed you up.

So she put her hand on Lummy, tried to get through to him. He was dressed, but might not have been. Lummy's kind was never ever born for clothes. At fourteen he looked more.

"Well," she said, sourer than she felt. "I'm not gunna cry over any sulky boy. Suit yourself."

She moved off.

As Dad had got out the old rattle-bones by now, Lum begun to clamber up. The back of the ute was at least private, though it wasn't no Customline.

The fact that Whalleys ran a Customline as well puzzled more unreasonable minds. Drawn up amongst the paspalum in front of Whalleys' shack, it looked stolen,

3 **inaccessible:** unzugänglich, abweisend.
7 **mug** (slang): Trottel.
8 **shickered** (Austral., slang): besoffen.
to bash s.o. up: jdn. zusammenschlagen.
14 **sulky:** verdrießlich, mißmutig.
suit yourself: mach, was du willst.
16 **rattle-bones:** etwa: Klapperkiste.
17 **to clamber:** (mühsam) klettern.
ute (Austral.): Kurzform von *utility truck:* Kombi.
18 **wasn't no:** *was no.*
Customline: Limousinentyp.
21 **paspalum:** australisches Sumpfgras.
shack: Schuppen.

and almost was – the third payment overdue. But would slither with ease a little longer to Barranugli, and snooze outside the Northern Hotel. Lum could have stood all day to admire their own two-tone car. Or would stretch out inside, his fingers at work on plastic flesh.

Now it was the ute for business. The bones of his buttocks bit into the boards. His father's meaty arm stuck out at the window, disgusting him. And soon the twins were squeezing from the rusty boiler. The taffy Gary – or was it Barry? – had fallen down and barked his knee.

"For Chrissake!" Mrs Whalley shrieked, and tossed her identical taffy hair.

Mrs Hogben watched those Whalleys leave.

"In a brick area, I wouldn't of thought," she remarked to her husband once again.

"All in good time, Myrtle," Councillor Hogben replied as before.

"Of course," she said, "if there are *reasons*."

Because councillors, she knew, did have reasons.

"But that home! And a Customline!"

The saliva of bitterness came in her mouth.

It was Daise who had said: I'm going to enjoy the good

2 **to slither:** gleiten.
to snooze: dösen.
4 **two-tone:** zweifarbig.
6 f. **buttocks** (pl., coll.): Hintern.
10 **to bark:** auf-, abschürfen.
15 **brick area:** hier: (besseres) Viertel mit Ziegelhäusern.
17 **all in good time:** alles zu seiner Zeit.
councillor: Ratsmitglied, Gemeinderat.
22 **saliva:** Speichel.

things of life – and died in that poky little hutch, with only a cotton frock to her back. While Myrtle had the liver-coloured brick home – not a single dampmark on the ceilings – she had the washing-machine, the septic, the TV, and the cream Holden Special, not to forget her husband. Les Hogben, the councillor. A builder into the bargain.

Now Myrtle stood amongst her things, and would have continued to regret the Ford the Whalleys hadn't paid for, if she hadn't been regretting Daise. It was not so much her sister's death as her life Mrs Hogben deplored. Still, everybody knew, and there was nothing you could do about it.

"Do you think anybody will come?" Mrs Hogben asked.

"What do you take me for?" her husband replied. "One of these cleervoyants?"

Mrs Hogben did not hear.

After giving the matter consideration she had advertised the death in the *Herald*:

MORROW, Daisy (Mrs), suddenly, at her residence,
Showground Road, Sarsaparilla.

1 **poky:** armselig.
hutch (coll.): Hütte, Verschlag.
2 **to one's back:** am Leibe.
3 **liver-coloured:** leberfarben, rotbraun.
dampmark: feuchte Stelle.
4 **septic:** *septic tank:* Faulbehälter.
5 **Holden Special:** australisches Autofabrikat bzw. -modell.
6 **builder:** Bauunternehmer.
6 f. **into the bargain:** obendrein.
11 **to deplore:** beklagen.
17 **cleervoyant:** *clairvoyant:* Hellseher.
22 **showground:** Rummelplatz, Kirmes.

There was nothing more you could put. It wasn't fair on Les, a public servant, to rake up relationships. And the *Mrs* – well, everyone had got into the habit when Daise started going with Cunningham. It seemed sort of natural as things dragged on and on. Don't work yourself up, Myrt, Daise used to say; Jack will when his wife dies. But it was Jack Cunningham who died first. Daise said: It's the way it happened, that's all.

"Do you think Ossie will come?" Councillor Hogben asked his wife slower than she liked.

"I hadn't thought about it," she said.

Which meant she had. She had, in fact, woken in the night, and lain there cold and stiff, as her mind's eye focused on Ossie's runny nose.

Mrs Hogben rushed at a drawer which somebody – never herself – had left hanging out. She was a thin woman, but wiry.

"Meg?" she called. "Did you polish your shoes?"

Les Hogben laughed behind his closed mouth. He always did when he thought of Daise's parting folly: to take up with that old scabby deadbeat Ossie from down at the showground. But who cared?

1 **to put:** hier: zum Ausdruck bringen.
2 **public servant:** jd. im öffentlichen Dienst.
to rake up: (alte Geschichten) aufrühren.
5 **to work o.s. up:** sich aufregen.
14 **to focus on s.th.:** sich auf etwas konzentrieren.
runny: triefend.
17 **wiry:** drahtig.
20 **parting:** hier: letzte(r, -s).
20 f. **to take up with s.o.** (coll.): mit jdm. anbändeln, sich mit jdm. einlassen.
21 **scabby** (coll.): räudig, schäbig.
deadbeat (Austral.): Habenichts, Strolch.

No one, unless her family.

Mrs Hogben dreaded the possibility of Ossie, a Roman Catholic for extra value, standing beside Daise's grave, even if nobody, even if only Mr Brickle saw.

Whenever the thought of Ossie Coogan crossed Councillor Hogben's mind he would twist the knife in his sister-in-law. Perhaps, now, he was glad she had died. A small woman, smaller than his wife, Daise Morrow was large by nature. Whenever she dropped in she was all around the place. Yarn her head off if she got the chance. It got so as Les Hogben could not stand hearing her laugh. Pressed against her in the hall once. He had forgotten that, or almost. How Daise laughed then. I'm not so short of men I'd pick me own brother-in-law. Had he pressed? Not all that much, not intentional, anyway. So the incident had been allowed to fade, dim as the brown-linoleum hall, in Councillor Hogben's mind.

"There's the phone, Leslie."

It was his wife.

"I'm too upset," she said, "to answer."

And began to cry.

Easing his crutch Councillor Hogben went into the hall.

It was good old Horrie Last.

3 **for extra value** (coll.): zu allem Unglück auch noch.
6 **to twist the knife in s.o.** (coll., fig.): etwa: jdn. als Feind behandeln, jdm. feindlich gesonnen sein.
9 **large:** großherzig.
to drop in: hereinschauen, vorbeikommen.
10 **to yarn one's head off** (coll.): bis zum Umfallen quasseln.
11 **to get so as** (coll.): so weit kommen, daß . . .
23 **crutch:** *crotch:* Schritt (Hose).

"Yairs . . . yairs . . ." said Mr Hogben, speaking into the telephone which his wife kept swabbed with Breath-o'-Pine. "Yairs . . . Eleven, Horrie . . . from Barranugli . . . from Jackson's Personal . . . Yairs, that's decent of you, Horrie."

"Horrie Last," Councillor Hogben reported to his wife, "is gunna put in an appearance."

If no one else, a second councillor for Daise. Myrtle Hogben was consoled.

What could you do? Horrie Last put down the phone. He and Les had stuck together. Teamed up to catch the more progressive vote. Hogben and Last had developed the shire. Les had built Horrie's home, Lasts had sold Hogbens theirs. If certain people were spreading the rumour that Last and Hogben had caused a contraction of the Green Belt, then certain people failed to realize the term itself implied flexibility.

"What did you tell them?" aked Mrs Last.

"Said I'd go," her husband said, doing things to the change in his pocket.

He was a short man, given to standing with his legs apart.

Georgina Last withheld her reply. Formally of interest,

1 **yairs** (Austral., coll.): (gedehnt gesprochenes) *yes*.
2 **to swab:** wischen.
2 f. **Breath-o'-Pine:** Markenname eines Putzmittels.
7 **to put in an appearance:** (persönlich) erscheinen.
11 **to stick together:** (fig.) zusammenhalten.
to team up (coll.): sich zusammentun, gemeinsame Sache machen.
13 **shire** (Austral.): Landkreis.
15 **contraction:** Einschränkung, Verkürzung.
16 **green belt:** Grüngürtel.
21 (*to be*) **given to doing s.th.:** etwas gern tun.

her shape suggested she had been made out of several scones joined together in the baking.

"Daise Morrow," said Horrie Last, "wasn't such a bad sort."

Mrs Last did not answer.

So he stirred the money in his pocket harder, hoping perhaps it would emulsify. He wasn't irritated, mind you, by his wife – who had brought him a parcel of property, as well as a flair for real estate – but had often felt he might have done a dash with Daise Morrow on the side. Wouldn't have minded betting old Les Hogben had tinkered a bit with his wife's sister. Helped her buy her home, they said. Always lights on at Daise's place after dark. Postman left her mail on the veranda instead of in the box. In summer, when the men went round to read the meters, she'd ask them in for a glass of beer. Daise knew how to get service.

Georgina Last cleared her throat.

"Funerals are not for women," she declared, and took up a cardigan she was knitting for a cousin.

"You didn't do your shoes!" Mrs Hogben protested.

"I did," said Meg. "It's the dust. Don't know why we

2 **scone:** weiches Teegebäck.
3 f. **not a bad sort** (coll.): keine so üble Type.
7 **to emulsify:** emulgieren, sich verflüssigen.
7 f. **mind you:** wohlgemerkt.
8 f. **parcel of property:** (ordentliches) Stück Grundbesitz.
9 **flair:** Spürsinn.
real estate: Immobilien.
10 f. **to do a dash on the side:** etwa: einen Seitensprung wagen.
12 **to tinker with s.o.:** mit jdm. herumfummeln.
15 f. **to read the meter:** den Zähler ablesen.
20 **cardigan:** Strickjacke.

bother to clean shoes at all. They always get dirty again."

She stood there looking awful in the awful school uniform. Her cheeks were hollow from what she read could only be despair.

"A person must keep to her principles," Mrs Hogben said, and added: "Dadda is bringing round the car. Where's your hat, dear? We'll be ready to leave in two minutes."

"Arr, Mum! The hat?"

That old school hat. It had shrunk already a year ago, but had to see her through.

"You wear it to church, don't you?"

"But this isn't church!"

"It's as good as. Besides, you owe it to your aunt," Mrs Hogben said, to win.

Meg went and got her hat. They were going out through the fuchsia bushes, past the plaster pixies, which Mrs Hogben had trained her child to cover with plastic at the first drops of rain. Meg Hogben hated the sight of those corny old pixies, even after the plastic cones had snuffed them out.

It was sad in the car, dreamier. As she sat looking out through the window, the tight panama perched on her

4 f. **from what she read ... be despair:** etwa: was nach ihrer Auslegung nur Verzweiflung sein konnte.
7 **dadda:** *daddy.*
12 **to see s.o. through:** jdm. reichen.
18 **pixy:** Gartenzwerg.
21 **corny:** kitschig.
cone: hier: (kegelförmige) Abdeckung, Mütze.
21 f. **to snuff out:** ersticken.
24 **panama:** Panamahut.
to perch: (hoch) sitzen.

head lost its power to humiliate. Her always persistent, grey eyes, under the line of dark fringe, had taken up the search again: she had never yet looked enough. Along the road they passed the house in which her aunt, they told her, had died. The small, pink tilted house, standing amongst the carnation plants, had certainly lost some of its life. Or the glare had drained the colour from it. How the mornings used to sparkle in which Aunt Daise went up and down between the rows, her gown dragging heavy with dew, binding with bast the fuzzy flowers by handfuls and handfuls. Auntie's voice clear as morning. No one, she called, could argue they look stiff when they're bunched tight eh Meg what would you say they remind you of? But you never knew the answers to the sort of things people asked. Frozen fireworks, Daise suggested. Meg loved the idea of it, she loved Daise. Not so frozen either, she dared. The sun getting at the wet flowers broke them up and made them spin.

And the clovy scent rose up in the stale-smelling car, and smote Meg Hogben, out of the reeling heads of flowers, their cold stalks dusted with blue. Then she knew

1 **to humiliate:** demütigen.
2 **fringe:** (Haar-)Fransen.
5 **tilted:** geneigt, schief, schräg.
6 **carnation:** Nelke.
10 **fuzzy:** struppig.
13 **to bunch:** zu einem Strauß binden.
eh: nicht wahr?
17 **to dare:** hier: dagegenhalten, behaupten.
18 **to spin:** (herum)wirbeln, kreisen.
19 **clovy:** gewürznelkenhaft, nelkenwürzig.
stale-smelling: muffig riechend.
20 **to smite:** entgegenschlagen, treffen.
to reel: schwanken, wirbeln.

she would write a poem about Aunt Daise and the carnations. She wondered she hadn't thought of it before.

At that point the passengers were used most brutally as the car entered on a chain of potholes. For once Mrs Hogben failed to invoke the Main Roads Board. She was asking herself whether Ossie could be hiding in there behind the blinds. Or whether, whether. She fished for her second handkerchief. Prudence had induced her to bring two – the good one with the lace insertion for use beside the grave.

"The weeds will grow like one thing," her voice blared, "now that they'll have their way."

Then she began to unfold the less important of her handkerchiefs.

Myrtle Morrow had always been the sensitive one. Myrtle had understood the Bible. Her needlework, her crochet doilies had taken prizes at country shows. No one had fiddled such pathos out of the pianola. It was Daise who loved flowers, though. It's a moss-rose, Daise had said, sort of rolling it round on her tongue, while she was still a little thing.

4 **to use:** behandeln.
5 **pothole:** Schlagloch.
6 **to invoke:** anrufen, beschwören.
Main Roads Board: Straßenbauamt.
9 **prudence:** Umsicht.
10 **lace insertion:** Spitzeneinsatz.
12 **like one thing** (coll.): drauflos.
to blare: posaunen, schmettern.
13 **to have one's way:** freie Bahn haben.
18 **crotchet doily:** Häkeldeckchen.
19 **to fiddle:** fingern.
pianola: automatisches Klavier.

When she had had her cry, Mrs Hogben remarked: "Girls don't know they're happy until it's too late." Thus addressed, the other occupants of the car did not answer. They knew they were not expected to. Councillor Hogben drove in the direction of Barranugli. He had arranged his hat before leaving. He removed a smile the mirror reminded him was there. Although he no longer took any risks in a re-election photograph by venturing out of the past, he often succeeded in the fleshy present. But now, in difficult circumstances, he was exercising his sense of duty. He drove, he drove, past the retinosperas, heavy with their own gold, past the lagerstroemias, their pink sugar running into mildew.

Down at the dump Whalleys were having an argument about whether the beer was to be drunk on arrival or after they had developed a thirst.

"Keep it, then!" Mum Whalley turned her back. "What was the point of buyin' it cold if you gotta wait till it hots up? Anyways," she said, "I thought the beer was an excuse for comin'."

"Arr, stuff it!" says Wal. "A dump's business, ain't it? With or without beer. Ain't it? Any day of the week."

He saw she had begun to sulk. He saw her rather long

3 **occupant:** Insasse.
12 **retinospera:** Zypressenart.
13 **lagerstroemia:** tropische Strauchart.
13 f. **mildew:** Mehltau.
19 f. **to hot up** (coll.): *to heat up*.
22 **stuff it** (slang): etwa: du kannst mich mal.
25 **to sulk:** schmollen.

breasts floating around inside her dress. Silly cow! He laughed. But cracked a bottle.

Barry said he wanted a drink.

You could hear the sound of angry suction as his mum's lips called off a swig.

"I'm not gunna stand by and watch any kid of mine," said the wet lips, "turn 'isself into a bloody dipso!"

Her eyes were at their blazing bluest. Perhaps it was because Wal Whalley admired his wife that he continued to desire her.

But Lummy pushed off on his own. When his mum went crook, and swore, he was too aware of the stumps of teeth, the rotting brown of nastiness. It was different, of course, if you swore yourself. Sometimes it was unavoidable.

Now he avoided by slipping away, between the old mattresses, and boots the sun had buckled up. Pitfalls abounded: the rusty traps of open tins lay in wait for guiltless ankles, the necks of broken bottles might have been prepared to gash a face. So he went thoughtfully,

2 **to crack a bottle** (coll.): eine Pulle aufmachen.
4 **suction:** Saugen.
5 **to call off s.th.** (coll.): etwas abbrechen.
swig: (kräftiger) Zug, Schluck.
7 f. **dipso:** *dipsomaniac:* periodisch Trunksüchtige(r), Quartalssäufer(in).
11 **to push off** (coll.): losziehen, abhauen.
11 f. **to go crook** (Austral., slang): ‚sauer' werden.
13 **nastiness:** Ekelhaftigkeit.
16 f. **mattress:** Matratze.
17 **to buckle up:** (ver)biegen, krümmen.
pitfall: Fallgrube.
18 **trap:** Klappe, Deckel.
20 **to gash:** aufschlitzen.

his feet scuffing the leaves of stained asbestos, crunching the torso of a celluloid doll. Here and there it appeared as though trash might win. The onslaught of metal was pushing the scrub into the gully. But in many secret, steamy pockets, a rout was in progress: seeds had been sown in the lumps of grey, disintegrating kapok and the laps of burst chairs, the coils of springs, locked in the spirals of wirier vines, had surrendered to superior resilience. Somewhere on the edge of the whole shambles a human ally, before retiring, had lit a fire, which by now the green had almost choked, leaving a stench of smoke to compete with the sicklier one of slow corruption.

Lum Whalley walked with a grace of which he himself had never been aware. He had had about enough of this rubbish jazz. He would have liked to know how to live

1 **to scuff:** aufscharren; streifen.
1 f. **to crunch:** zermalmen.
2 **torso:** Rumpf.
3 **trash:** Abfall, Müll.
onslaught: Ansturm.
4 **scrub:** Gestrüpp, Buschwerk.
gully: Rinne, Senke.
5 **steamy:** dampfig.
pocket: Loch, Nest, Kessel; hier auch: Winkel, Ecke.
rout: (wilde) Zusammenrottung.
6 **kapok:** Kapok (baumwollartiges Füllmaterial für Polster).
7 **lap:** hier: Sitzfläche.
coil of spring: Sprungfeder.
9 **resilience:** Spannkraft.
9 f. **shambles:** Trümmerfeld.
11 **to choke:** ersticken.
12 **sickly:** krankhaft, eklig.
16 **rubbish:** Müll.
jazz: Krampf, Blödsinn.

neat. Like Darkie Black. Everything in its place in the cabin of Darkie's trailer. Suddenly his throat yearned for Darkie's company. Darkie's hands, twisting the wheel, appeared to control the whole world.
A couple of strands of barbed wire separated Sarsaparilla dump from Sarsaparilla cemetery. The denominations were separated too, but there you had to tell by the names, or by the angels and things the RIPs went in for. Over in what must have been the Church of England Alf Herbert was finishing Mrs Morrow's grave. He had reached the clay, and the going was heavy. The clods fell resentfully.
If what they said about Mrs Morrow was true, then she had lived it up all right. Lum Whalley wondered what, supposing he had met her walking towards him down a bush track, smiling. His skin tingled. Lummy had never done a girl, although he pretended he had, so as to hold his own with the kids. He wondered if a girl, if that sourpuss Meg Hogben. Would of bitten as likely as not.

1 **neat:** ordentlich.
2 **cabin:** Fahrer-, Führerhaus.
trailer: Lastzug (in Australien oft mit mehreren Anhängern).
to yearn for s.th.: sich nach etwas sehnen.
5 **strand:** (Draht-)Litze.
barbed wire: Stacheldraht.
6 f. **denomination:** Konfession.
8 **RIP:** Abk. für *Requiescat in Pace* (Lat.): Ruhe in Frieden.
9 **Church of England:** Anglikanische Kirche.
11 **the going was heavy:** es war eine Schinderei.
clod: Erdklumpen.
14 **to live it up** (slang): kein Kind von Traurigkeit sein.
16 **to tingle:** prickeln, kribbeln.
16 f. **to do s.o.** (slang): es mit jdm. treiben.
17 f. **to hold one's own:** sich behaupten.
18 f. **sourpuss:** Miesepeter.

Lummy felt a bit afraid, and returned to thinking of Darkie Black, who never talked about things like that. Presently he moved away. Alf Herbert, leaning on his shovel, could have been in need of a yarn. Lummy was not prepared to yarn. He turned back into the speckled bush, into the pretences of a shade. He lay down under a banksia, and opened his fly to look at himself. But pretty soon got sick of it.

The procession from Barranugli back to Sarsaparilla was hardly what you would have called a procession: the Reverend Brickle, the Hogbens' Holden, Horrie's Holden, following the smaller of Jackson's hearses. In the circumstances they were doing things cheap – there was no reason for splashing it around. At Sarsaparilla Mr Gill joined in, sitting high in that old Chev. It would have been practical, Councillor Hogben sighed, to join the hearse at Sarsaparilla. Old Gill was only there on account of Daise being his customer for years. A grocer lacking in enterprise, Daise had stuck to him, she said, because she liked him. Well, if that was what you put first, but where did it get you?

4 **yarn:** Schwatz.
5 **speckled:** gesprenkelt, gefleckt.
6 **pretence:** Anschein.
7 **banksia:** immergrüner Strauch in Australien.
fly: Hosenschlitz.
9 **procession:** hier: Leichenzug.
11 **Reverend:** Hochwürden.
12 f. **hearse:** Leichenwagen.
14 **to splash around** (coll.): (Geld) mit vollen Händen ausgeben.
16 **Chev:** Kurzform von *Chevrolet* (amerikanisches Autofabrikat).

At the last dip before the cemetery a disembowelled mattress from the dump had begun to writhe across the road. It looked like a kind of monster from out of the depths of somebody's mind, the part a decent person ignored.

"Ah, dear! At the cemetery too!" Mrs Hogben protested. "I wonder the Council," she added, in spite of her husband.

"All right, Myrtle," he said between his teeth. "I made a mental note."

Councillor Hogben was good at that.

"And the Whalleys on your own doorstep," Mrs Hogben moaned.

The things she had seen on hot days, in front of their kiddies too.

The hearse had entered the cemetery gate. They had reached the bumpy stage, toppling over the paspalum clumps, before the thinner, bush grass. All around, the leaves of the trees presented so many grey blades. Not even a magpie to put heart into a Christian. But Alf Herbert came forward, his hands dusted with yellow clay, to

1 **dip:** Gefälle, Senke.
to disembowel: ausweiden, ausnehmen.
2 **to writhe:** sich krümmen, winden.
7 **council:** Stadtverwaltung.
9 f. **to make a mental note:** sich etwas vormerken.
12 **on one's own doorstep:** vor der eigenen Tür.
15 **kiddie:** Diminutiv zu *kid.*
17 **bumpy:** holprig.
to topple: wackeln, kippen.
18 **clump:** Büschel.
20 **magpie:** Elster (in Australien mit ihrem frühmorgendlichen Gesang assoziiert).
to put heart into s.o.: jdm. Mut machen.

guide the hearse between the Methoes and the Presbyterians, onto Church of England ground.

Jolting had shaken Mrs Hogben's grief up to the surface again. Mr Brickle was impressed. He spoke for a moment of the near and dear. His hands were kind and professional in helping her out.

But Meg jumped. And landed. It was a shock to hear a stick crack so loud. Perhaps it was what Mum would have called irreverent. At the same time her banana-coloured panama fell off her head into the tussocks.

It was really a bit confusing at the grave. Some of the men helped with the coffin, and Councillor Last was far too short.

Then Mrs Hogben saw, she saw, from out of the lace handkerchief, it was that Ossie Coogan she saw, standing the other side of the grave. Had old Gill given him a lift? Ossie, only indifferently buttoned, stood snivelling behind the mound of yellow clay.

Nothing would have stopped his nose. Daise used to say: You don't want to be frightened, Ossie, not when I'm here, see? But she wasn't any longer. So now he was afraid. Excepting Daise, Protestants had always frightened him. Well, I'm nothing, she used to say, nothing that you could pigeonhole, but love what we are given to love.

1 **Metho** (Austral., coll.): Kurzform von *Methodist.*
3 **to jolt:** rütteln.
5 **the near and dear:** (fig.) die Nahestehenden.
9 **irreverent:** respektlos.
10 **tussock:** (Gras-)Büschel.
17 **to snivel:** schniefen.
18 **mound:** Erdhügel.
24 **to pigeonhole:** einordnen, abstempeln.

Myrtle Hogben was ropable, if only because of what Councillor Last must think. She would have liked to express her feelings in words, if she could have done so without giving offence to God. Then the ants ran up her legs, for she was standing on a nest, and her body cringed before the teeming injustices.

Daise, she had protested the day it all began, whatever has come over you? The sight of her sister had made her run out leaving the white sauce to burn. Wherever will you take him? He's sick, said Daise. *But you can't*, Myrtle Hogben cried. For there was her sister Daise pushing some old deadbeat in a barrow. All along Showground Road people had come out of homes to look. Daise appeared smaller pushing the wheelbarrow down the hollow and up the hill. Her hair was half uncoiled. *You can't! You can't!* Myrtle called. But Daise could, and did.

When all the few people were assembled at the graveside in their good clothes, Mr Brickle opened the book, though his voice soon suggested he needn't have.

"I am the resurrection and the life," he said.

1 **ropable** (Austral.): ärgerlich.
4 **to give offence to s.o.:** jds. Mißfallen erregen.
6 **to cringe:** sich krümmen, winden.
to teem: wimmeln.
13 **barrow:** *wheelbarrow:* Schubkarre.
16 **hollow:** Mulde, Senke.
to uncoil: abwickeln, lösen, entflechten.
20 **graveside:** Rand des Grabes (wo die Trauernden stehen).
23 **resurrection:** Auferstehung. Die hier und im folgenden zitierten Bibelverse und Gebetzeilen entstammen hauptsächlich der »Begräbnisordnung« des *Book of Common Prayer.*

And Ossie cried. Because he didn't believe it, not when it came to the real thing.

He looked down at the coffin, which was what remained of what he knew. He remembered eating a baked apple, very slowly, the toffee on it. And again the dark of the horse-stall swallowed him up, wherc he lay hopeless amongst the shit, and her coming at him with the barrow. What do you want? he asked straight out. I came down to the showground, she said, for a bit of honest-to-God manure, I've had those fertilizers, she said, and what are you, are you sick? I live 'ere, he said. And began to cry, and rub the snot from his snivelly nose. After a bit Daise said: We're going back to my place, What's-yer-name – Ossie. The way she spoke he knew it was true. All the way up the hill in the barrow the wind was giving his eyes gyp, and blowing his thin hair apart. Over the years he had come across one or two lice in his hair, but thought, or hoped he had got rid of them by the time Daise took him up. As she pushed and struggled with the barrow, sometimes she would lean forward, and he felt her warmth, her firm diddies pressed against his back.

"Lord, let me know mine end, and the number of my

2 **the real thing** (coll.): das Eigentliche.
4 **baked apple:** Bratapfel.
5 **toffee:** Karamel.
6 **horse-stall:** Pferdebox.
9 f. **honest-to-God** (coll.): richtig, anständig.
10 **manure:** Dung; Dünger.
fertilizer: Kunstdünger.
12 **snot:** Rotz.
16 **to give gyp** (coll.): schwer zu schaffen machen.
17 **lice:** Plural von *louse*.
21 **diddies:** *titties* (vulg.): Titten.

days: that I may be certified how long I have to live," Mr Brickle read.

Certified was the word, decided Councillor Hogben looking at that old Ossie.

Who stood there mumbling a few Aspirations, very quiet, on the strength of what they had taught him as a boy.

When all this was under way, all these words of which, she knew, her Auntie Daise would not have approved, Meg Hogben went and got beneath the strands of wire separating the cemetery from the dump. She had never been to the dump before, and her heart was lively in her side. She walked shyly through the bush. She came across an old suspender-belt. She stumbled over a blackened primus.

She saw Lummy Whalley then. He was standing under a banksia, twisting at one of its dead heads.

Suddenly they knew there was something neither of them could continue to avoid.

"I came here to the funeral," she said.

She sounded, well, almost relieved.

"Do you come here often?" she asked.

"Nah," he answered, hoarse. "Not here. To dumps, yes."

1 **to certify** (arch.): versichern, kundtun.
5 **to mumble:** murmeln.
aspiration: etwa: Anrufung, Stoßgebet.
6 **on the strength of s.th.:** kraft, aufgrund einer Sache.
14 **suspender-belt:** Strumpfhalter.
15 **primus:** *primus stove:* Primuskocher (Spirituskocher).
17 **dead:** abgestorben, welk.
23 **nah:** *no*.
hoarse: heiser, rauh.

But her intrusion had destroyed the predetermined ceremony of his life, and caused a trembling in his hand.

"Is there anything to see?" she asked.

"Junk," he said. "Same old junk."

"Have you ever looked at a dead person?"

Because she noticed the trembling of his hand.

"No," he said. "Have you?"

She hadn't. Nor did it seem probable that she would have to now. Not as they began breathing evenly again.

"What do you do with yourself?" he asked.

Then, even though she would have liked to stop herself, she could not. She said: "I write poems. I'm going to write one about my Aunt Daise, like she was, gathering carnations early in the dew."

"What'll you get out of that?"

"Nothing," she said, "I suppose."

But it did not matter.

"What other sorts of pomes do you write?" he asked, twisting at last the dead head of the banksia off.

"I wrote one," she said, "about the things in a cupboard. I wrote about a dream I had. And the smell of rain. That was a bit too short."

He began to look at her then. He had never looked into the eyes of a girl. They were grey and cool, unlike the hot or burnt-out eyes of women.

"What are you going to be?" she asked.

1 **predetermined:** vorherbestimmt.
5 **junk:** Gerümpel, Plunder, (sperriger) Müll.
12 **What do you do with yourself?:** Was treibst du so?
17 **to get s.th. out of s.th. else:** etwas von einer Sache haben.
28 **to be going to be:** (später) einmal werden.

"I dunno."

"You're not a white-collar type."

"Eh?"

"I mean, you're not for figures, and books, and banks and offices," she said.

He was too disgusted to agree.

"I'm gunna have me own truck. Like Mr Black. Darkie's got a trailer."

"What?"

"Well," he said, "a semi-trailer."

"Oh," she said, more diffident.

"Darkie took me on a trip to Maryborough. It was pretty tough goin'. Sometimes we drove right through the night. Sometimes we slept on the road. Or in places where you get rooms. Gee, it was good though, shootin' through the country towns at night."

She saw it. She saw the people standing at their doors, frozen in the blocks of yellow light. The rushing of the night made the figures forever still. All around she could feel the furry darkness, as the semi-trailer roared and bucked, its skeleton of coloured lights. While in the cabin, in which they sat, all was stability and order. If she glanced sideways she could see how his taffy hair shone when raked by the bursts of electric light. They had

1 **dunno:** *don't know.*
2 **white-collar type:** Angestelltentyp (mit sauberem Kragen).
10 **semi-trailer:** Sattelschlepper, -anhänger.
11 **diffident:** schüchtern, scheu.
12 **Maryborough:** Stadt im angrenzenden Staat Victoria.
13 **to be tough going** (coll.): ein Schlauch, eine Plackerei sein.
15 **gee:** Ausruf; etwa: Mann!
20 **furry:** pelzartig.
21 **to buck:** bocken, rucken.
24 **to rake:** durchstöbern, absuchen.

brought cases with tooth-brushes, combs, one or two things – the pad on which she would write the poem somewhere when they stopped in the smell of sunlight dust ants. But his hands had acquired such mastery over the wheel, it appeared this might never happen. Nor did she care.

"This Mr Black", she said, her mouth getting thinner, "does he take you with him often?"

"Only once interstate," said Lummy, pitching the banksia head away. "Once in a while short trips."

As they drove they rocked together. He had never been closer to anyone than when bumping against Darkie's ribs. He waited to experience again the little spasm of gratitude and pleasure. He would have liked to wear, and would in time, a striped sweatshirt like Darkie wore.

"I'd like to go in with Darkie," he said, "when I get a trailer of me own. Darkie's the best friend I got."

With a drawnout shiver of distrust she saw the darker hands, the little black hairs on the backs of the fingers.

"Oh, well," she said, withdrawn, "praps you will in the end," she said.

2 **pad:** Schreibblock.
9 **interstate:** über die Bundesstaatsgrenze.
to pitch: schleudern.
10 **once in a while:** ab und zu.
12 **to bump:** stoßen; purzeln.
13 **spasm:** Krampf, Anfall.
17 **to go in with s.o.** (coll.): sich mit jdm. zusammentun.
19 **drawnout:** anhaltend, lang.
22 **praps:** *perhaps.*

On the surrounding graves the brown flowers stood in their jars of browner water. The more top-heavy, plastic bunches had been slapped down by a westerly, but had not come to worse grief than to lie strewn in pale disorder on the uncharitable granite chips.

The heat made Councillor Last yawn. He began to read the carved names, those within sight at least, some of which he had just about forgot. He almost laughed once. If the dead could have sat up in their graves there would have been an argument or two.

"In the midst of life we are in death," said the parson bloke.

JACK CUNNINGHAM
BELOVED HUSBAND OF FLORENCE MARY,

read Horrie Last.

Who would have thought Cunningham, straight as a silky-oak, would fall going up the path to Daise Morrow's place. Horrie used to watch them together, sitting awhile on the veranda before going in to their tea. They made no bones about it, because everybody knew. Good teeth Cunningham had. Always a white, well-ironed shirt. Wonder which of the ladies did the laundry. Florence Mary was an invalid, they said. Daise Morrow

2 **top-heavy:** kopflastig.
3 **to slap down:** hinknallen, umstoßen.
westerly: Westwind.
4 **strewn:** verstreut.
5 **granite chip:** Granitsplitter.
17 **silky-oak:** Australische Silbereiche, Seideneiche (bis 50 m hoher Baum der Gattung Grevillea).
20 **to make no bones about s.th.:** keinen Hehl aus etwas machen.
22 **to do the laundry:** die (schmutzige) Wäsche waschen.

liked to laugh with men, but for Jack Cunningham she had a silence, promising intimacies at which Horrie Last could only guess, whose own private life had been lived in almost total darkness.

Good Christ, and then there was Ossie. The woman could only have been at heart a perv of a kind you hadn't heard about.

"Forasmuch as it hath pleased Almighty God of his great mercy to take unto himself the soul ..." read Mr Brickle.

As it was doubtful who should cast the earth, Mr Gill the grocer did. They heard the handful rattle on the coffin.

Then the tears truly ran out of Ossie's scaly eyes. Out of darkness. Out of darkness Daise had called: What's up, Ossie, you don't wanta cry. I got the cramps, he answered. They were twisting him. The cramps? she said drowsily. Or do you imagine? If it isn't the cramps it's something else. Could have been. He'd take Daise's word for it. He was never all that bright since he had the meningitis. Tell you what, Daise said, you come in here, into my bed, I'll warm you, Os, in a jiffy. He listened in

6 **perv** (Austral., slang): Perverse(r).
8 **forasmuch as:** insofern, da, nachdem.
hath (arch.): *has.*
14 **scaly:** grindig.
15 **what's up** (coll.): was is' los?
16 **cramp:** Krampf.
18 **drowsily** (adv.): schläfrig.
19 f. **to take s.o.'s word for it:** nicht an jds. Worten zweifeln, sich auf jdn. verlassen.
21 **meningitis:** Hirnhautentzündung.
tell you what (coll.): paß auf!, hör mal!
22 **in a jiffy:** im Nu.

the dark to his own snivelling. Arr, Daise, I couldn't, he said, I couldn't get a stand, not if you was to give me the jackpot, he said. She sounded very still then. He lay and counted the throbbing of the darkness. Not like that, she said – she didn't laugh at him as he had half expected – besides, she said, it only ever really comes to you once. That way. And at once he was parting the darkness, bumping and shambling, to get to her. He had never known it so gentle. Because Daise wasn't afraid. She ran her hands through his hair, on and on like water flowing. She soothed the cramps out of his legs. Until in the end they were breathing in time. Dozing. Then the lad Ossie Coogan rode again down from the mountain, the sound of the snaffle in the blue air, the smell of sweat from under the saddlecloth, towards the great, flowing river. He rocked and flowed with the motion of the strong, never-ending river, burying his mouth in brown cool water, to drown would have been worth it.

Once during the night Ossie had woken, afraid the distance might have come between them. But Daise was still holding him against her breast. If he had been differ-

2 **to get a stand** (vulg.): einen hoch kriegen.
3 **jackpot:** Haupttreffer, Bombenerfolg.
4 **to throb:** beben, pulsieren.
8 **to bump:** rumpeln, holpern.
to shamble: torkeln.
11 **to soothe:** (Schmerz) lindern.
12 **in time:** im Takt.
13 **to doze:** schlummern.
lad: (junger) Bursche.
14 **snaffle:** Trense (Pferdezaum).
15 **saddlecloth:** Satteldecke.

ent, say. Ossie's throat had begun to wobble. Only then, Daise, Daise might have turned different. So he nuzzled against the warm darkness, and was again received.

"If you want to enough, you can do what you want," Meg Hogben insisted.

She had read it in a book, and wasn't altogether convinced, but theories sometimes come to the rescue.

"If you want," she said, kicking a hole in the stony ground.

"Not everything you can't."

"You can!" she said. "But you can!"

She who had never looked at a boy, not right into one, was looking at him as never before.

"That's a lot of crap," he said.

"Well," she admitted, "there are limits."

It made him frown. He was again suspicious. She was acting clever. All those pomes.

But to reach understanding she would have surrendered her cleverness. She was no longer proud of it.

"And what'll happen if you get married? Riding around the country in a truck. How'll your wife like it? Stuck at home with a lot of kids."

"Some of 'em take the wife along. Darkie takes his missus and kids. Not always, like. But now and again. On short runs."

1 **say** (coll.): angenommen.
to wobble: zittern.
3 **to nuzzle against s.th.:** sich an etwas kuscheln.
15 **crap** (coll.): Quatsch, Stuß.
24 f. **missus** (coll.): ‚bessere Hälfte', Alte.
25 **like:** sozusagen, versteht sich.

"You didn't tell me Mr Black was married."

"Can't tell you everything, can I? Not at once."

The women who sat in the drivers' cabins of the semi-trailers he saw as predominantly thin and dark. They seldom returned glances, but wiped their hands on Kleenex, and peered into little mirrors, waiting for their men to show up again. Which in time they had to. So he walked across from the service station, to take possession of his property. Sauntering, frowning slightly, touching the yellow stubble on his chin, he did not bother to look. Glanced sideways perhaps. She was the thinnest, the darkest he knew, the coolest of all the women who sat looking out from the cabin windows of the semi-trailers.

In the meantime they strolled a bit, amongst the rusty tins at Sarsaparilla dump. He broke a few sticks and threw away the pieces. She tore off a narrow leaf and smelled it. She would have liked to smell Lummy's hair.

"Gee, you're fair," she had to say.

"Some are born fair," he admitted.

He began pelting a rock with stones. He was strong, she saw. So many discoveries in a short while were making her tremble at the knees.

And as they rushed through the brilliant light, roaring and lurching, the cabin filled with fair-skinned, taffy children, the youngest of whom she was protecting by

4 **predominantly** (adv.): vorwiegend.
8 **service station:** Tankstelle.
9 **to saunter:** schlendern, bummeln.
10 **stubble:** Stoppel(n).
22 **to pelt:** bewerfen.
26 **to lurch:** schlingern.

holding the palm of her hand behind his neck, as she had noticed women do. Occupied in this way, she almost forgot Lum at times, who would pull up, and she would climb down, to rinse the nappies in tepid water, and hang them on a bush to dry.

"All these pomes and things," he said, "I never knew a clever person before."

"But clever isn't any different," she begged, afraid he might not accept her peculiarity and power.

She would go with a desperate wariness from now. She sensed that, if not in years, she was older than Lum, but this was the secret he must never guess: that for all his strength, all his beauty, she was, and must remain the stronger.

"What's that?" he asked, and touched.

But drew back his hand in self-protection.

"A scar," she said. "I cut my wrist opening a tin of condensed milk."

For once she was glad of the paler seam in her freckled skin, hoping that it might heal a breach.

And he looked at her out of his hard blue Whalley eyes. He liked her. Although she was ugly, and clever, and a girl.

"Condensed milk on bread," he said, "that's something I could eat till I bust."

3 **to pull up:** anhalten.
4 **to rinse:** spülen.
nappie: Windel.
tepid: lauwarm.
10 **wariness:** Behutsamkeit.
19 **seam:** Schramme.
20 **breach:** Bruchstelle, Verletzung.
25 **to bust:** platzen.

"Oh, yes!" she agreed.

She did honestly believe, although she had never thought of it before.

Flies clustered in irregular jet embroideries on the backs of best suits. Nobody bothered any longer to shrug them off. As Alf Herbert grunted against the shovelfuls, dust clogged increasingly, promises settled thicker. Although they had been told they might expect Christ to redeem, it would have been no less incongruous if He had appeared out of the scrub to perform on altars of burning sandstone a sacrifice for which nobody had prepared them. In any case, the mourners waited – they had been taught to accept whatever might be imposed – while the heat stupefied the remnants of their minds, and inflated their Australian fingers into foreign-looking sausages.

Myrtle Hogben was the first to protest. She broke down – into the wrong handkerchief. *Who shall change our vile body?* The words were more than her decency could bear.

4 **to cluster:** Trauben bilden, sich scharen.
jet embroidery: Gagatstickerei (*jet:* Gagat, als Schmuckstein verwendete Pechkohle).
5 **best suit** (coll.): Sonntagsanzug.
5 f. **to shrug off:** (durch Achselzucken) abschütteln.
6 **to grunt:** murren.
7 **to clog:** sich zusammenballen.
8 **to redeem:** erlösen.
9 **incongruous:** unpassend.
14 **to stupefy:** betäuben.
14 f. **to inflate:** aufblähen, anschwellen lassen.
19 **vile:** gemein, schlecht; nichtswürdig.

"Easy on it," her husband whispered, putting a finger under her elbow.

She submitted to his sympathy, just as in their life together she had submitted to his darker wishes. Never wanting more than peace, and one or two perquisites.

A thin woman, Mrs Hogben continued to cry for all the wrongs that had been done her. For Daise had only made things viler. While understanding, yes, at moments. It was girls who really understood, not even women – sisters, sisters. Before events whirled them apart. So Myrtle Morrow was again walking through the orchard, and Daise Morrow twined her arm around her sister; confession filled the air, together with a scent of crushed, fermenting apples. Myrtle said: Daise, there's something I'd like to do, I'd like to chuck a lemon into a Salvation Army tuba. Daise giggled. You're a nut, Myrt, she said. But never *vile*. So Myrtle Hogben cried. Once, only once she had thought how she'd like to push someone off a cliff, and watch their expression as it happened. But Myrtle had not confessed that.

So Mrs Hogben cried, for those things she was unable to confess, for anything she might not be able to control.

As the blander words had begun falling, *Our Father*, that

1 (*go*) **easy on it** (coll.): nimm's nicht so schwer!
5 **perquisite:** persönliches Vorrecht.
12 **to twine:** schlingen.
14 **to ferment:** gären.
15 **to chuck:** schmeißen.
16 **Salvation Army:** Heilsarmee.
to giggle: kichern.
nut (coll.): Verrückte(r), Spinner(in).
24 **bland:** mild.

she knew by heart, *our daily bread*, she should have felt comforted. She should of. Should of.

Where was Meg, though?

Mrs Hogben separated herself from the others. Walking stiffly. If any of the men noticed, they took it for granted she had been overcome, or wanted to relieve herself. She would have liked to relieve herself by calling: "Margaret Meg wherever don't you hear me Me-ehg?" drawing it out thin in anger. But could not cut across a clergyman's words. So she stalked. She was not unlike a guinea-hen, its spotted silk catching on a strand of barbed-wire.

When they had walked a little farther, round and about, anywhere, they overheard voices.

"What's that?" asked Meg.

"Me mum and dad," Lummy said. "Rousin' about somethun or other."

Mum Whalley had just found two bottles of unopened beer. Down at the dump. Waddayaknow. Must be something screwy somewhere.

"Could of put poison in it," her husband warned.

"Poison? My arse!" she shouted. "That's because *I* found it!"

9 **to cut across s.th.:** gegen etwas verstoßen.
10 **to stalk:** (einher)stolzieren.
11 **guinea-hen:** Perlhuhn.
to catch on s.th.: in etwas hängenbleiben, sich in etwas verfangen.
13 **round and about:** rundherum, überall und nirgends.
14 **to overhear:** (zufällig) hören.
16 **to rouse** (Austral., slang): zanken, keifen.
19 **whaddayaknow:** *what do you know:* na so was.
20 **screwy:** faul, verquer.
22 **my arse** (vulg.): leck mich!

"Whoever found it," he said, "who's gunna drink a coupla bottlesa hot beer?"

"I am!" she said.

"When what we brought was good an' cold?"

He too was shouting a bit. She behaved unreasonable at times.

"Who wanted ter keep what we brought? Till it got good an' hot!" she shrieked.

Sweat was running down both the Whalleys.

Suddenly Lum felt he wanted to lead this girl out of earshot. He had just about had the drunken sods. He would have liked to find himself walking with his girl over mown lawn, like at the Botanical Gardens, a green turf giving beneath their leisured feet. Statues pointed a way through the glare, to where they finally sat, under enormous shiny leaves, looking out at boats on water. They unpacked their cut lunch from its layers of fresh tissue-paper.

"They're rough as bags," Lummy explained.

"I don't care," Meg Hogben assured.

Nothing on earth could make her care – was it more, or was it less?

10 f. **out of earshot:** außer Hörweite.
11 **to have had s.th.** (coll.): die Nase voll von etwas haben.
just about: so ziemlich.
sod (slang): ‚Schwein'.
13 **to mow:** mähen.
14 **turf:** Grasnarbe.
to give: nachgeben, federn.
14 f. **leisured:** müßig, gemächlich.
18 **cut lunch:** aus Schnitten bestehender (Mittags-)Imbiß.
layer: Lage, Schicht.
18 f. **tissue-paper:** Seidenpapier.

She walked giddily behind him, past a rusted fuel-stove, over a field of deathly feltex. Or ran, or slid, to keep up. Flowers would have wilted in her hands, if she hadn't crushed them brutally, to keep her balance. Somewhere in their private labyrinth Meg Hogben had lost her hat.

When they were farther from the scene of anger, and a silence of heat had descended again, he took her little finger, because it seemed natural to do so, after all they had experienced. They swung hands for a while, according to some special law of motion.

Till Lum Whalley frowned, and threw the girl's hand away.

If she accepted his behaviour it was because she no longer believed in what he did, only in what she knew he felt. That might have been the trouble. She was so horribly sure, he would have to resist to the last moment of all. As a bird, singing in the prickly tree under which they found themselves standing, seemed to cling to the air. Then his fingers took control. She was amazed at the hardness of his boy's body. The tremors of her flinty skin, the membrane of the white sky appalled him. Before fright and expectation melted their mouths. And they took little grateful sips of each

1 **giddily** (adv.): schwindelig.
fuel-stove: Heizofen.
2 **feltex:** Filzteppich.
3 **to wilt:** (ver)welken.
18 **prickly:** stachelig, dornig.
21 **tremors** (pl.): Zittern.
22 **flinty:** kieselhart, steinern.
membrane: Membran(e), (zarte, dünne) Haut.
22 f. **to appal:** erschrecken.
24 **sip:** Schlückchen.

other. Holding up their throats in between. Like birds drinking.

Ossie could no longer see Alf Herbert's shovel working at the earth.

"Never knew a man cry at a funeral," Councillor Hogben complained, very low, although he was ripe enough to burst.

If you could count Ossie as a man, Councillor Last suggested in a couple of noises.

But Ossie could not see or hear, only Daise, still lying on that upheaval of a bed. Seemed she must have burst a button, for her breasts stood out from her. He would never forget how they laboured against the heavy yellow morning light. In the early light, the flesh turned yellow, sluggish. What's gunna happen to me, Daisy? It'll be decided, Os, she said, like it is for any of us. I ought to know, she said, to tell you, but give me time to rest a bit, to get me breath. Then he got down on his painful knees. He put his mouth to Daise's neck. Her skin tasted terrible bitter. The great glistening river, to which the lad Ossie Coogan had ridden jingling down from the mountain, was slowing into thick, yellow mud. Himself an old, scabby man attempting to refresh his forehead in the last pothole.

Mr Brickle said: *"We give thee hearty thanks for that it*

11 **upheaval:** Durcheinander.
15 **sluggish:** träge, schwerfällig.
21 **to glisten:** glitzern.
25 **pothole:** hier: Wasserloch.
26 **thee** (arch.): *you.*

hath pleased thee to deliver this our sister out of the miseries of this sinful world."

"No! No!" Ossie protested, so choked nobody heard, though it was vehement enough in its intention.

As far as he could understand, nobody wanted to be delivered. Not him, not Daise, anyways. When you could sit together by the fire on winter nights baking potatoes under the ashes.

It took Mrs Hogben some little while to free her *crêpe de Chine* from the wire. It was her nerves, not to mention Meg on her mind. In the circumstances she tore herself worse, and looked up to see her child, just over there, without shame, in a rubbish tip, kissing with the Whalley boy. What if Meg was another of Daise? It was in the blood, you couldn't deny.

Mrs Hogben did not exactly call, but released some kind of noise from her extended throat. Her mouth was too full of tongue to find room for words as well.

Then Meg looked. She was smiling.

She said: "Yes, Mother."

She came and got through the wire, tearing herself also a little.

Mrs Hogben said, and her teeth clicked: "You chose the likeliest time. Your aunt hardly in her grave.

1 **to deliver:** erlösen.
9 f. **crêpe de Chine** (Fr.): Chinakrepp (Seidengewebe); hier: Bluse, Kleid o. ä. aus Chinakrepp.
11 **Meg on her mind:** die Sorge um Meg.
13 **tip:** Müllkippe.
14 **another of:** *another.*
23 **to click:** klappern, aufeinanderschlagen.
24 **likely:** passend.

Though, of course, it is only your aunt, if anyone, to blame."

The accusations were falling fast. Meg could not answer. Since joy had laid her open, she had forgotten how to defend herself.

"If you were a little bit younger" – Mrs Hogben lowered her voice because they had begun to approach the parson – "I'd break a stick on you, my girl."

Meg tried to close her face, so that nobody would see inside.

"What will they say?" Mrs Hogben moaned. "What ever will happen to us?"

"What, Mother?" Meg asked.

"You're the only one can answer that. And someone else."

Then Meg looked over her shoulder and recognized the hate which, for a while, she had forgotten existed. And at once her face closed up tight, like a fist. She was ready to protect whatever justly needed her protection.

Even if their rage, grief, contempt, boredom, apathy, and sense of injustice had not occupied the mourners, it is doubtful whether they would have realized the dead woman was standing amongst them. The risen dead – that was something which happened, or didn't happen, in the Bible. Fanfares of light did not blare for a loose woman in floral cotton. Those who had known her

3 **to fall:** hier: hereinbrechen, hageln.
4 **to lay open:** (fig.) entblößen.
23 **to rise:** (von den Toten) auferstehen.
25 f. **loose woman:** loses Weibsstück.
26 **floral:** geblümt.

remembered her by now only fitfully in some of the wooden attitudes of life. How could they have heard, let alone believed in, her affirmation? Yet Daise Morrow continued to proclaim.

Listen, all of you, I'm not leaving, except those who want to be left, and even those aren't so sure – they might be parting with a bit of themselves. Listen to me, all you successful no-hopers, all of you who wake in the night, jittery because something may be escaping you, or terrified to think there may never have been anything to find. Come to me, you sour women, public servants, anxious children, and old scabby, desperate men. . . .

Physically small, words had seemed too big for her. She would push back her hair in exasperation. And take refuge in acts. Because her feet have been planted in the earth, she would have been the last to resent its pressure now, while her always rather hoarse voice continued to exhort in borrowed syllables of dust.

Truly, we needn't experience tortures, unless we build chambers in our minds to house instruments of hatred in. Don't you know, my darling creatures, that death isn't death, unless it's the death of love? Love should be the greatest explosion it is reasonable to expect. Which sends us whirling, spinning, creating millions of other worlds. Never destroying.

1 **fitfully** (adv.): unregelmäßig, launenhaft.
2 f. **let alone:** geschweige denn.
8 **no-hoper** (Austral.): Ohnemichel (Anhänger des Ohne-mich-Standpunkts); Nichtsnutz.
jittery (slang): durchgedreht, bibbernd.
14 **exasperation:** Verärgerung.
18 **to exhort:** ermahnen.
21 **creature:** hier: Mitmensch.

From the fresh mound which they had formed unimaginatively in the shape of her earthly body, she persisted in appealing to them.

I will comfort you. If you will let me. Do you understand?

But nobody did, as they were only human.

For ever and ever. And ever.

Leaves quivered lifted in the first suggestion of a breeze.

So the aspirations of Daise Morrow were laid alongside her small-boned wrists, smooth thighs and pretty ankles. She surrendered at last to the formal crumbling which, it was hoped, would make an honest woman of her.

But had not altogether died.

Meg Hogben had never exactly succeeded in interpreting her aunt's messages, nor could she have witnessed the last moments of the burial, because the sun was dazzling her. She did experience, however, along with a shiver of recollected joy, the down laid against her cheek, a little breeze trickling through the moist roots of her hair, as she got inside the car, and waited for whatever next.

Well, they had dumped Daise.

Somewhere the other side of the wire there was the sound of smashed glass and discussion.

10 **alongside:** neben, Seite an Seite mit.
11 **small-boned:** feingliedrig.
thigh: (Ober-)Schenkel.
19 **down:** Flaum.
20 **to trickle:** sickern.
23 **to dump:** abladen, loswerden, wegschaffen.
25 **to smash:** zerschmettern.

Councillor Hogben went across to the parson and said the right kind of things. Half-turning his back he took a note or two from his wallet, and immediately felt disengaged. If Horrie Last had been there Les Hogben would have gone back at this point and put an arm around his mate's shoulder, to feel whether he was forgiven for unorthodox behaviour in a certain individual – no relation, mind you, but. In any case Horrie had driven away.

Horrie drove, or flew, across the dip in which the dump joined the cemetery. For a second Ossie Coogan's back flickered inside a spiral of dust.

Ought to give the coot a lift, Councillor Last suspected, and wondered, as he drove on, whether a man's better intentions were worth, say, half a mark in the event of their remaining unfulfilled. For by now it was far too late to stop, and there was that Ossie, in the mirror, turning off the road towards the dump, where, after all, the bugger belonged.

All along the road, stones, dust, and leaves, were settling back into normally unemotional focus. Seated in his high Chev, Gill the grocer, a slow man, who carried his change in a little, soiled canvas bag, looked ahead through thick lenses. He was relieved to realize he would reach home almost on the dot of three-thirty, and

3 f. **disengaged:** befreit, entbunden.
6 **mate:** Kumpel.
12 **to flicker:** aufflackern, zucken.
13 **coot** (coll.): Schwachkopf, Trottel.
19 **bugger** (vulg.): Knilch, Scheißkerl.
23 **canvas bag:** Leinentasche, -beutel.
24 **lenses:** Brillengläser.
25 **on the dot of . . .:** Punkt . . . Uhr.

his wife pour him his cup of tea. Whatever he understood was punctual, decent, docketed.

As he drove, prudently, he avoided the mattress the dump had spewed, from under the wire, half across the road. Strange things had happened at the dump on and off, the grocer recollected. Screaming girls, their long tight pants ripped to tatters. An arm in a sugar-bag, and not a sign of the body that went with it. Yet some found peace amongst the refuse: elderly derelict men, whose pale, dead, fish eyes never divulged anything of what they had lived, and women with blue, metho skins, hanging around the doors of shacks put together from sheets of bark and rusty iron. Once an old downandout had crawled amongst the rubbish apparently to rot, and did, before they sent for the constable, to examine what seemed at first a bundle of stinking rags.

Mr Gill accelerated judiciously.

They were driving. They were driving.

Alone in the back of the ute, Lum Whalley sat forward on the empty crate, locking his hands between his

2 **to docket:** etikettieren.
4 **to spew:** speien.
5 f. **on and off:** ab und zu.
7 **pants** (pl.): Hose.
tatters (pl.): Fetzen.
9 **refuse:** Müll, Abfall.
derelict: heruntergekommen, verwahrlost.
10 **to divulge:** verbreiten, preisgeben, verraten.
11 **metho** (Austral., slang): *metholated spirits* (pl.): Methylalkohol.
13 **downandout:** Penner.
17 **to accelerate:** beschleunigen, Gas geben.
judiciously (adv.): wohlüberlegt.
20 **crate:** Kasten.

knees, as he forgot having seen Darkie do. He was completely independent now. His face had been reshaped by the wind. He liked that. It felt good. He no longer resented the junk they were dragging home, the rust flaking off at his feet, the roll of mouldy feltex trying to fur his nostrils up. Nor his family – discussing, or quarrelling, you could never tell – behind him in the cabin. The Whalleys were in fact singing. One of their own versions. They always sang their own versions, the two little boys joining in.

"Show me the way to go home,
I'm not too tired for bed.
I had a little drink about an hour ago,
And it put ideas in me head . . ."

Suddenly Mum Whalley began belting into young Gary – or was it Barry?
"Wadda *you* know, eh? Wadda *you?*"
"What's bitten yer?" her husband shouted. "Can't touch a drop without yer turn nasty!"
She didn't answer. He could tell a grouse was coming,

2 **to reshape:** neu formen, umbilden.
5 **to flake off:** abblättern.
mouldy: modrig, muffig.
6 **to fur s.th. up:** etwas (mit einem pelzigen Belag) überziehen.
nostril: Nasenloch.
11 ff. **"Show me the way to go home":** Abwandlung eines 1925 kreierten, populären englischen Tanzparty-Schlußsongs von Irving King.
15 **to belt into s.o.** (coll.): auf jdn. ein-, losprügeln.
18 **What's bitten yer?:** Was is' in dich gefahren?
18 f. **to touch a drop** (coll.): Alkohol anrühren, einen ‚heben'.
19 **nasty:** garstig.
20 **grouse:** Gemecker.

though. The little boy had started to cry, but only as a formality.

"It's that bloody Lummy," Mrs Whalley complained.

"Why pick on Lum?"

"Give a kid all the love and affection, and waddayaget?"

Wal grunted. Abstractions always embarrassed him.

Mum Whalley spat out of the window, and the spit came back at her.

"Arrrr!" she protested.

And fell silenter. It was not strictly Lum, not if you was honest. It was nothing. Or everything. The grog. You was never ever gunna touch it no more. Until you did. And that bloody Lummy, what with the caesar and all, you was never ever going again with a man.

"That's somethink a man don't understand."

"What?" asked Wal.

"A caesar."

"Eh?"

You just couldn't discuss with a man. So you had to get into bed with him. Grogged up half the time. That was how she copped the twins, after she had said never ever.

"Stop cryun, for Chrissake!" Mum Whalley coaxed, touching the little boy's blowing hair.

Everything was sad.

4 **to pick on s.o.** (coll.): auf jdm. herumhacken.
12 **grog** (Austral., coll.): Schnaps.
14 **what with:** in Anbetracht.
caesar (coll.): *caesarian:* Kaiserschnitt.
21 **grogged up** (slang): vollgesoffen.
22 **to cop** (slang): abbekommen.
24 **to coax:** gut zureden.

"Wonder how often they bury someone alive," she said.

Taking a corner in his cream Holden Councillor Hogben felt quite rakish, but would restrain himself at the critical moment from skidding the wrong side of the law.

They were driving and driving, in long, lovely bursts, and at the corners, in semicircular swirls.

On those occasions in her life when she tried to pray, begging for an experience, Meg Hogben would fail, but return to the attempt with clenched teeth. Now she did so want to think of her dead aunt with love, and the image blurred repeatedly. She was superficial, that was it. Yet, each time she failed, the landscape leaped lovingly. They were driving under the telephone wires. She could have translated any message into the language of peace. The wind burning, whenever it did not cut cold, left the stable things alone: the wooden houses stuck beside the road, the trunks of willows standing round the brown saucer of a dam. Her too candid, grey eyes seemed to have deepened, as though to accommodate all she still had to see, feel.

4 **rakish:** flott, keck.
5 **to skid:** rutschen, schliddern, schleudern.
7 **burst:** Schub.
8 **semicircular:** halbkreisförmig.
swirl: Wirbel.
11 **to clench:** (Zähne) zusammenpressen.
13 **to blur:** verschwimmen.
superficial: oberflächlich.
18 **stable:** standfest.
20 **saucer:** Untertasse.
candid: aufrichtig, freimütig.

It was lovely curled on the back seat, even with Mum and Dad in front.

"I haven't forgotten, Margret," Mum called over her shoulder.

Fortunately Dadda wasn't interested enough to inquire.

"Did Daise owe anything on the home?" Mrs Hogben asked. "She was never at all practical."

Councillor Hogben cleared his throat.

"Give us time to find out," he said.

Mrs Hogben respected her husband for the things which she, secretly, did not understand: Time the mysterious, for instance, Business, and worst of all, the Valuer General.

"I wonder Jack Cunningham," she said, "took up with Daise. He was a fine man. Though Daise had a way with her."

They were driving. They were driving.

When Mrs Hogben remembered the little ring in plaited gold.

"Do you think those undertakers are honest?"

"Honest?" her husband repeated.

A dubious word.

"Yes," she said. "That ring that Daise."

You couldn't very well accuse. When she had plucked up the courage she would go down to the closed house. The thought of it made her chest tighten. She would go

1 **to curl:** sich (gemütlich) einrollen.
13 f. **Valuer General:** amtlicher Taxator.
16 **to have a way with o.s.:** das gewisse Etwas haben.
21 **undertaker:** Bestattungsunternehmer.
23 **dubious:** zweifelhaft.
25 f. **to pluck up courage:** Mut fassen.

inside, and feel her way into the back corners of drawers, where perhaps a twist of tissue-paper. But the closed houses of the dead frightened Mrs Hogben, she had to admit. The stuffiness, the light strained through brown holland. It was as if you were stealing, though you weren't.

And then those Whalleys creeping up.

They were driving and driving, the ute and the sedan almost rubbing on each other.

"No one who hasn't had a migraine," cried Mrs Hogben, averting her face, "can guess what it feels like."

Her husband had heard that before.

"It's a wonder it don't leave you," he said. "They say it does when you've passed a certain age."

Though they weren't passing the Whalleys he would make every effort to throw the situation off. Wal Whalley leaning forward, though not so far you couldn't see the hair bursting out of the front of his shirt. His wife thumping his shoulder. They were singing one of their own versions. Her gums all watery.

So they drove and drove.

"I could sick up, Leslie," Mrs Hogben gulped, and fished for her lesser handkerchief.

2 **twist:** Knäuel.
4 **stuffiness:** Stickigkeit.
to strain: filtern.
4 f. **brown holland:** ungebleichte Leinwand.
7 **to creep up:** heranschleichen.
8 **sedan:** Limousine.
11 **to avert:** abwenden.
19 **to thump:** puffen, knuffen.
20 **gums** (pl.): Zahnfleisch.
22 **to sick up** (coll.): spucken, brechen.
to gulp: schlucken.

The Whalley twins were laughing through their taffy forelocks.
At the back of the ute that sulky Lum turned towards the opposite direction. Meg Hogben was looking her farthest off. Any sign of acknowledgment had been so faint the wind had immediately blown it off their faces. As Meg and Lummy sat, they held their sharp, but comforting knees. They sank their chins as low as they would go. They lowered their eyes, as if they had seen enough for the present, and wished to cherish what they knew.
The warm core of certainty settled stiller as driving faster the wind payed out the telephone wires the fences fences the flattened heads of grey grass always raising themselves again again again

2 **forelock:** Stirnlocke.
11 **core:** Kern, Innerstes.
12 **to pay out:** (Seil) abwickeln, ablaufen lassen.

Peter Carey

American Dreams

No one can, to this day, remember what it was we did to offend him. Dyer the butcher remembers a day when he gave him the wrong meat and another day when he served someone else first by mistake. Often when Dyer gets drunk he recalls this day and curses himself for his foolishness. But no one seriously believes that it was Dyer who offended him.

But one of us did something. We slighted him terribly in some way, this small meek man with the rimless glasses and neat suit who used to smile so nicely at us all. We thought, I suppose, he was a bit of a fool and sometimes he was so quiet and grey that we ignored him, or forgot that he was there at all.

When I was a boy I often stole apples from the trees at his house up in Mason's Lane. He often saw me. No, that's not correct. Let me say I often sensed that he saw me. I sensed him peering out from behind the lace curtains of his house. And I was not the only one. Many of us came to take his apples, alone and in groups, and it is

7 **to recall s.th.:** sich an etwas erinnern.
10 **to slight:** geringschätzig behandeln, vernachlässigen.
11 **meek:** sanft(mütig), bescheiden.
rimless: randlos.
12 **neat:** ordentlich.
13 **a bit of a fool:** etwas närrisch.
14 **grey** (fig.): trübe, düster.

possible that he chose to exact payment for all these apples in his own peculiar way.

Yet I am sure it wasn't the apples.

What has happened is that we all, all eight hundred of us, have come to remember small transgressions against Mr Gleason who once lived amongst us.

My father, who has never borne malice against a single living creature, still believes that Gleason meant to do us well, that he loved the town more than any of us. My father says we have treated the town badly in our minds. We have used it, this little valley, as nothing more than a stopping place. Somewhere on the way to somewhere else. Even those of us who have been here many years have never taken the town seriously. Oh yes, the place is pretty. The hills are green and the woods thick. The stream is full of fish. But it is not where we would rather be.

For years we have watched the films at the Roxy and dreamed, if not of America, then at least of our capital city. For our own town, my father says, we have nothing but contempt. We have treated it badly, like a whore. We have cut down the giant shady trees in the main street to make doors for the school house and seats for the football pavilion. We have left big holes all over the countryside from which we have taken brown coal and given back nothing.

1 **to exact:** eintreiben, verlangen, fordern.
5 **transgression:** Übertretung, Verstoß.
7 **to bear malice:** arglistig sein.
8 f. **to do s.o. well** (coll.): jdn. gut behandeln.
12 **stopping place:** Haltestelle, Station.
21 **whore:** Hure.
24 **pavilion:** (Sportplatz-)Pavillon; Klubhaus.

The commercial travellers who buy fish and chips at George the Greek's care for us more than we do, because we all have dreams of the big city, of wealth, of modern houses, of big motor cars: American dreams, my father has called them.

Although my father ran a petrol station he was also an inventor. He sat in his office all day drawing strange pieces of equipment on the back of delivery dockets. Every spare piece of paper in the house was covered with these little drawings and my mother would always be very careful about throwing away any piece of paper no matter how small. She would look on both sides of any piece of paper very carefully and always preserved any that had so much as a pencil mark.

I think it was because of this that my father felt that he understood Gleason. He never said as much, but he inferred that he understood Gleason because he, too, was concerned with similar problems. My father was working on plans for a giant gravel crusher, but occasionally he would become distracted and become interested in something else.

There was, for instance, the time when Dyer the butcher bought a new bicycle with gears, and for a while my father talked of nothing else but the gears. Often I would see him across the road squatting down beside Dyer's bicycle as if he were talking to it.

1 **commercial traveller:** Handlungsreisender.
8 **delivery docket:** Lieferschein.
16 **to say as much:** direkt sagen.
17 **to infer:** andeuten.
19 **gravel crusher:** Kiesbrecher (Zerkleinerungsmaschine).
23 **gears:** Gänge, Gangschaltung.
25 **to squat down:** sich niederhocken.

We all rode bicycles because we didn't have the money for anything better. My father did have an old Chev truck, but he rarely used it and it occurs to me now that it might have had some mechanical problem that was impossible to solve, or perhaps it was just that he was saving it, not wishing to wear it out all at once. Normally, he went everywhere on his bicycle and, when I was younger, he carried me on the cross bar, both of us dismounting to trudge up the hills that led into and out of the main street. It was a common sight in our town to see people pushing bicycles. They were as much a burden as a means of transport.

Gleason also had his bicycle and every lunchtime he pushed and pedalled it home from the shire offices to his little weatherboard house out at Mason's Lane. It was a three-mile ride and people said that he went home for lunch because he was fussy and wouldn't eat either his wife's sandwiches or the hot meal available at Mrs Lessing's cafe.

But while Gleason pedalled and pushed his bicycle to and from the shire offices everything in our town proceeded as normal. It was only when he retired that things began to go wrong.

Because it was then that Mr Gleason started supervising

2 **Chev:** Kurzform von *Chevrolet* (amerikanisches Autofabrikat).
6 **to wear s.th. out:** etwas kaputtmachen.
8 **cross bar:** (Fahrrad-)Stange.
9 **to trudge:** stapfen.
14 **to pedal:** strampeln, radeln.
shire offices (pl., Austral.): Landkreisamt.
15 **weatherboard:** Schindelbrett.
17 **fussy:** wählerisch.
24 **to supervise:** beaufsichtigen.

the building of the wall around the two-acre plot up on Bald Hill. He paid too much for this land. He bought it from Johnny Weeks, who now, I am sure, believes the whole episode was his fault, firstly for cheating Gleason, secondly for selling him the land at all. But Gleason hired some Chinese and set to work to build his wall. It was then that we knew that we'd offended him. My father rode all the way out to Bald Hill and tried to talk Mr Gleason out of his wall. He said there was no need for us to build walls. That no one wished to spy on Mr Gleason or whatever he wished to do on Bald Hill. He said no one was in the least bit interested in Mr Gleason. Mr Gleason, neat in a new sportscoat, polished his glasses and smiled vaguely at his feet. Bicycling back, my father thought that he had gone too far. Of course we had an interest in Mr Gleason. He pedalled back and asked him to attend a dance that was to be held on the next Friday, but Mr Gleason said he didn't dance.

"Oh well," my father said, "any time, just drop over."

Mr Gleason went back to supervising his family of Chinese labourers on his wall.

Bald Hill towered high above the town and from my

1 **two-acre:** zwei Acre groß (*acre:* Flächenmaß; 1 a entspricht etwa 4047 m²).
plot: Grundstück, Parzelle.
2 **bald:** kahl.
6 **to set to work to do s.th.:** sich daran machen, etwas zu tun.
9 **to talk s.o. out of s.th.:** jdm. etwas ausreden, jdn. von etwas abbringen.
11 **to spy on s.o.:** jdm. nachspionieren.
12 f. **in the least bit:** (auch nur) im geringsten.
14 **sportscoat:** Sportsakko.
20 **to drop over** (coll.): rüberkommen.

father's small filling station you could sit and watch the wall going up. It was an interesting sight. I watched it for two years, while I waited for customers who rarely came. After school and on Saturdays I had all the time in the world to watch the agonizing progress of Mr Gleason's wall. It was as painful as a clock. Sometimes I could see the Chinese labourers running at a jogtrot carrying bricks on long wooden planks. The hill was bare, and on this bareness Mr Gleason was, for some reason, building a wall.

In the beginning people thought it peculiar that someone would build such a big wall on Bald Hill. The only thing to recommend Bald Hill was the view of the town, and Mr Gleason was building a wall that denied that view. The top soil was thin and bare clay showed through in places. Nothing would ever grow there. Everyone assumed that Gleason had simply gone mad and after the initial interest they accepted his madness as they accepted his wall as they accepted Bald Hill itself.

Occasionally someone would pull in for petrol at my father's filling station and ask about the wall and my father would shrug and I would see, once more, the strangeness of it.

"A house?" the stranger would ask. "Up on that hill?"

1 **filling station:** Tankstelle.
5 **agonizing:** qualvoll.
7 **at a jogtrot:** im (gemächlichen) Trab.
9 **bareness:** Kahlheit.
15 **top soil:** Muttererde.
18 **initial:** anfänglich.
21 **to pull in:** hineinfahren; anhalten.

"No," my father would say, "chap named Gleason is building a wall."

And the strangers would want to know why, and my father would shrug and look up at Bald Hill once more. "Damned if I know," he'd say.

Gleason still lived in his old house at Mason's Lane. It was a plain weatherboard house with a rose garden at the front, a vegetable garden down the side, and an orchard at the back.

At night we kids would sometimes ride out to Bald Hill on our bicycles. It was an agonizing, muscle-twitching ride, the worst part of which was a steep, unmade road up which we finally pushed our bikes, our lungs rasping in the night air. When we arrived we found nothing but walls. Once we broke down some of the brickwork and another time we threw stones at the tents where the Chinese labourers slept. Thus we expressed our frustration at this inexplicable thing.

The wall must have been finished on the day before my twelfth birthday. I remember going on a picnic birthday party up to Eleven Mile Creek and we lit a fire and cooked chops at a bend in the river from where it was possible to see the walls on Bald Hill. I remember stand-

1 **chap:** Kerl.

5 (*I'm*) **damned if I know:** keine Ahnung, verdammt noch mal, hab nicht die leiseste Ahnung.

12 **muscle-twitching:** an den Muskeln zerrend, anstrengend.

14 **to rasp:** rasseln (Atem).

16 **brickwork:** Mauerwerk.

19 **inexplicable:** unerklärlich.

22 **creek:** Flüßchen.

23 **chop:** Kotelett.

ing with a hot chop in my hand and someone saying, "Look, they're leaving!"

We stood on the creek bed and watched the Chinese labourers walking their bicycles slowly down the hill. Someone said they were going to build a chimney up at the mine at A.1 and certainly there is a large brick chimney there now, so I suppose they built it.

When the word spread that the walls were finished most of the town went up to look. They walked around the four walls which were as interesting as any other brick walls. They stood in front of the big wooden gates and tried to peer through, but all they could see was a small blind wall that had obviously been constructed for this special purpose. The walls themselves were ten feet high and stopped with broken glass and barbed wire. When it became obvious that we were not going to discover the contents of the enclosure, we all gave up and went home.

Mr Gleason had long since stopped coming into town. His wife came instead, wheeling a pram down from Mason's Lane to Main Street and filling it with groceries and meat (they never bought vegetables, they grew their own) and wheeling it back to Mason's Lane. Sometimes you would see her standing with the pram halfway up the Gell Street hill. Just standing there, catching her breath. No one asked her about the wall. They knew she wasn't responsible for the wall and they felt sorry for

8 **word:** Nachricht.
13 **blind:** (architektonisch) funktionslos; verdeckt.
15 **barbed wire:** Stacheldraht.
17 **enclosure:** Einfriedung.
20 **pram:** Kinderwagen.

her, having to bear the burden of the pram and her husband's madness. Even when she began to visit Dixon's hardware and buy plaster of paris and tins of paint and waterproofing compound, no one asked her what these things were for. She had a way of averting her eyes that indicated her terror of questions. Old Dixon carried the plaster of paris and the tins of paint out to her pram for her and watched her push them away. "Poor woman," he said, "poor bloody woman."

From the filling station where I sat dreaming in the sun, or from the enclosed office where I gazed mournfully at the rain, I would see, occasionally, Gleason entering or leaving his walled compound, a tiny figure way up on Bald Hill. And I'd think "Gleason", but not much more.

Occasionally strangers drove up there to see what was going on, often egged on by locals who told them it was a Chinese temple or some other silly thing. Once a group of Italians had a picnic outside the walls and took photographs of each other standing in front of the closed door. God knows what they thought it was.

But for five years between my twelfth and seventeenth birthdays there was nothing to interest me in Gleason's walls. Those years seem lost to me now and I can remember very little of them. I developed a crush on

3 **hardware:** Eisenwaren.
plaster of Paris: Gips(mörtel).
4 **waterproofing compound:** wasserdicht machendes Gemisch.
5 **to avert:** abwenden.
13 **compound:** (umschlossenes) Areal, Gelände.
17 **to egg on:** anstacheln.
local: Ortsansässige(r).
25 **to develop a crush on s.o.:** sich in jdn. verknallen.

Susy Markin and followed her back from the swimming pool on my bicycle. I sat behind her in the pictures and wandered past her house. Then her parents moved to another town and I sat in the sun and waited for them to come back.

We became very keen on modernization. When coloured paints became available the whole town went berserk and brightly coloured houses blossomed overnight. But the paints were not of good quality and quickly faded and peeled, so that the town looked like a garden of dead flowers. Thinking of those years, the only real thing I recall is the soft hiss of bicycle tyres on the main street. When I think of it now it seems very peaceful, but I remember then that the sound induced in me a feeling of melancholy, a feeling somehow mixed with the early afternoons when the sun went down behind Bald Hill and the town felt as sad as an empty dance hall on a Sunday afternoon.

And then, during my seventeenth year, Mr Gleason died. We found out when we saw Mrs Gleason's pram parked out in front of Phonsey Joy's Funeral Parlour. It looked very sad, that pram, standing by itself in the windswept street. We came and looked at the pram and felt sad for Mrs Gleason. She hadn't had much of a life.

Phonsey Joy carried old Mr Gleason out to the cemetery

2 **pictures** (pl.): Kino, Film.
7 f. **to go berserk:** wild werden.
10 **to peel:** abblättern.
11 **dead:** abgestorben, verwelkt.
12 **tyre:** *tire:* Reifen.
21 **funeral parlour:** Bestattungsinstitut.
23 **windswept:** windgepeitscht.

by the Parwan Railway Station and Mrs Gleason rode behind in a taxi. People watched the old hearse go by and thought, "Gleason", but not much else.

And then, less than a month after Gleason had been buried out at the lonely cemetery by the Parwan Railway Station, the Chinese labourers came back. We saw them push their bicycles up the hill. I stood with my father and Phonsey Joy and wondered what was going on.

And then I saw Mrs Gleason trudging up the hill. I nearly didn't recognize her, because she didn't have her pram. She carried a black umbrella and walked slowly up Bald Hill and it wasn't until she stopped for breath and leant forward that I recognized her.

"It's Mrs Gleason," I said, "with the Chinese."

But it wasn't until the next morning that it became obvious what was happening. People lined the main street in the way they do for a big funeral but, instead of gazing towards the Grant Street corner, they all looked up at Bald Hill.

All that day and all the next we gathered to watch the destruction of the walls. We saw the Chinese labourers darting to and fro, but it wasn't until they knocked down a large section of the wall facing the town that we realized there really was something inside. It was impossible to see what it was, but there was something there. People stood and wondered and pointed out Mrs Glea-

2 **hearse:** Leichenwagen.
17 **to line:** (Straße) säumen.
23 **to dart:** flitzen.
to and fro: hin und her.
27 **to point s.o. out:** auf jdn. aufmerksam machen.

son to each other as she went to and fro supervising the work.

And finally, in ones and twos, on bicycles and on foot, the whole town moved up to Bald Hill. Mr Dyer closed up his butcher shop and my father got out the old Chev truck and we finally arrived up at Bald Hill with twenty people on board. They crowded into the back tray and hung onto the running boards and my father grimly steered his way through the crowds of bicycles and parked just where the dirt track gets really steep. We trudged up this last steep track, never for a moment suspecting what we would find at the top.

It was very quiet up there. The Chinese labourers worked diligently, removing the third and fourth walls and cleaning the bricks which they stacked neatly in big piles. Mrs Gleason said nothing either. She stood in the only remaining corner of the walls and looked defiantly at the townspeople who stood open-mouthed where another corner had been.

And between us and Mrs Gleason was the most incredibly beautiful thing I had ever seen in my life. For one moment I didn't recognize it. I stood open-mouthed, and breathed the surprising beauty of it. And then I realized it was our town. The buildings were two feet high and they were a little rough but very correct. I saw

3 **in ones and twos** (pl.): einzeln und zu zweit.
7 **on board:** an Bord, im Fahrzeug.
back tray: (offene) Ladefläche.
8 **running board:** Trittbrett.
10 **dirt track:** unbefestigte Straße, Feldweg.
15 **to stack:** stapeln.
17 **defiantly** (adv.): trotzig, keck.
23 **to breathe s.th.:** (fig.) etwas einatmen, in sich aufnehmen.

Mr Dyer nudge my father and whisper that Gleason had got the faded "U" in the BUTCHER sign of his shop.
I think at that moment everyone was overcome with a feeling of simple joy. I can't remember ever having felt so uplifted and happy. It was perhaps a childish emotion but I looked up at my father and saw a smile of such warmth spread across his face that I knew he felt just as I did. Later he told me that he thought Gleason had built the model of our town just for this moment, to let us see the beauty of our own town, to make us proud of ourselves and to stop the American Dreams we were so prone to. For the rest, my father said, was not Gleason's plan and he could not have foreseen the things that happened afterwards.

I have come to think that this view of my father's is a little sentimental and also, perhaps, insulting to Gleason. I personally believe that he knew everything that would happen. One day the proof of my theory may be discovered. Certainly there are in existence some personal papers, and I firmly believe that these papers will show that Gleason knew exactly what would happen.
We had been so overcome by the model of the town that we hadn't noticed what was the most remarkable thing of all. Not only had Gleason built the houses and the shops of our town, he had also peopled it. As we tip-toed into the town we suddenly found ourselves. "Look," I said to Mr Dyer, "there you are."

1 **to nudge:** anstoßen, stupsen.
5 **to uplift:** erheben, erbauen.
11 f. **to be prone to s.th.:** empfänglich für etwas sein, zu etwas neigen.
25 **to tip-toe:** auf Zehenspitzen gehen.

And there he was, standing in front of his shop in his apron. As I bent down to examine the tiny figure I was staggered by the look on its face. The modelling was crude, the paint work was sloppy, and the face a little too white, but the expression was absolutely perfect: those pursed, quizzical lips and the eyebrows lifted high. It was Mr Dyer and no one else on earth.

And there beside Mr Dyer was my father, squatting on the footpath and gazing lovingly at Mr Dyer's bicycle's gears, his face marked with grease and hope.

And there was I, back at the filling station, leaning against a petrol pump in an American pose and talking to Brian Sparrow who was amusing me with his clownish antics.

Phonsey Joy standing beside his hearse. Mr Dixon sitting inside his hardware store. Everyone I knew was there in that tiny town. If they were not in the streets or in their backyards they were inside their houses, and it didn't take very long to discover that you could lift off the roofs and peer inside.

We tip-toed around the streets peeping into each other's windows, lifting off each other's roofs, admiring each other's gardens, and, while we did it, Mrs Gleason

3 **staggered:** verblüfft.
4 **crude:** roh, grob.
sloppy: nachlässig, schludrig.
6 **to purse:** (Lippen) schürzen, (Mund) spitzen.
quizzical: spöttisch.
11 **grease:** Schmierfett, Öl.
13 **petrol pump:** Zapfsäule.
14 f. **clownish:** närrisch.
15 **antics** (pl.): Mätzchen.

slipped silently away down the hill towards Mason's Lane. She spoke to nobody and nobody spoke to her.

I confess that I was the one who took the roof from Cavanagh's house. So I was the one who found Mrs Cavanagh in bed with young Craigie Evans.

I stood there for a long time, hardly knowing what I was seeing. I stared at the pair of them for a long, long time. And when I finally knew what I was seeing I felt such an incredible mixture of jealousy and guilt and wonder that I didn't know what to do with the roof.

Eventually it was Phonsey Joy who took the roof from my hands and placed it carefully back on the house, much, I imagine, as he would have placed the lid on a coffin. By then other people had seen what I had seen and the word passed around very quickly.

And then we all stood around in little groups and regarded the model town with what could only have been fear. If Gleason knew about Mrs Cavanagh and Craigie Evans (and no one else had), what other things might he know? Those who hadn't seen themselves yet in the town began to look a little nervous and were unsure of whether to look for themselves or not. We gazed silently at the roof and felt mistrustful and guilty.

We all walked down the hill then, very quietly, the way people walk away from a funeral, listening only to the crunch of the gravel under our feet while the women had trouble with their high-heeled shoes.

11 **eventually** (adv.): schließlich.
13 **much as:** ziemlich so, wie ...
15 **to pass around:** die Runde machen.
23 **mistrustful:** argwöhnisch.
26 **crunch:** knirschen.
27 **high-heeled:** hochhackig.

The next day a special meeting of the shire council passed a motion calling on Mrs Gleason to destroy the model town on the grounds that it contravened building regulations.

It is unfortunate that this order wasn't carried out before the city newspapers found out. Before another day had gone by the government had stepped in.

The model town and its model occupants were to be preserved. The minister for tourism came in a large black car and made a speech to us in the football pavilion. We sat on the high, tiered seats eating potato chips while he stood against the fence and talked to us. We couldn't hear him very well, but we heard enough. He called the model town a work of art and we stared at him grimly. He said it would be an invaluable tourist attraction. He said tourists would come from everywhere to see the model town. We would be famous. Our businesses would flourish. There would be work for guides and interpreters and caretakers and taxi drivers and people selling soft drinks and ice creams.

The Americans would come, he said. They would visit our town in buses and in cars and on the train. They

1 **special meeting:** Sondersitzung.
shire council (Austral.): Landkreisrat.
2 **to pass a motion:** einen Antrag annehmen, verabschieden.
3 **to contravene s.th.:** gegen etwas verstoßen.
3 f. **building regulations:** Bauvorschriften.
5 **to carry out an order:** eine Anordnung ausführen.
7 **to step in:** einschreiten.
8 **occupant:** Bewohner.
11 **tiered:** übereinander gereiht.
19 **interpreter:** Dolmetscher.
caretaker: Hausmeister, -verwalter.
20 **soft:** alkoholfrei.

would take photographs and bring wallets bulging with dollars. American dollars.

We looked at the minister mistrustfully, wondering if he knew about Mrs Cavanagh, and he must have seen the look because he said that certain controversial items would be removed, had already been removed. We shifted in our seats, like you do when a particularly tense part of a film has come to its climax, and then we relaxed and listened to what the minister had to say. And we all began, once more, to dream our American dreams.

We saw our big smooth cars cruising through cities with bright lights. We entered expensive night-clubs and danced till dawn. We made love to women like Kim Novak and men like Rock Hudson. We drank cocktails. We gazed lazily into refrigerators filled with food and prepared ourselves lavish midnight snacks which we ate while we watched huge television sets on which we would be able to see American movies free of charge and forever.

The minister, like someone from our American dreams, re-entered his large black car and cruised slowly from our humble sportsground, and the newspaper men arrived and swarmed over the pavilion with their cameras and note books. They took photographs of us and pho-

1 **wallet:** Brieftasche.
to bulge with s.th.: mit etwas vollgestopft sein, vor etwas bersten.
5 **controversial:** umstritten.
8 **tense:** spannungsgeladen.
climax: Höhepunkt.
12 **to cruise:** kreuzen, herumfahren.
17 **lavish:** üppig, reichlich.
19 **free of charge:** kostenlos.

tographs of the models up on Bald Hill. And the next day we were all over the newspapers. The photographs of the model people side by side with photographs of the real people. And our names and ages and what we did were all printed there in black and white.

They interviewed Mrs Gleason but she said nothing of interest. She said the model town had been her husband's hobby.

We all felt good now. It was very pleasant to have your photograph in the paper. And, once more, we changed our opinion of Gleason. The shire council held another meeting and named the dirt track up Bald Hill, "Gleason Avenue". Then we all went home and waited for the Americans we had been promised.

It didn't take long for them to come, although at the time it seemed an eternity, and we spent six long months doing nothing more with our lives than waiting for them.

Well, they did come. And let me tell you how it has all worked out for us.

The Americans arrive every day in buses and cars and sometimes the younger ones come on the train. There is now a small airstrip out near the Parwan cemetery and they also arrive there, in small aeroplanes. Phonsey Joy drives them to the cemetery where they look at Gleason's grave and then up to Bald Hill and then down to the town. He is doing very well from it all. It is good to see someone doing well from it. Phonsey is becoming a big man in town and is on the shire council.

On Bald Hill there are half a dozen telescopes through

20 **to work out:** sich anlassen, entwickeln.
23 **airstrip:** Behelfsflughafen, Landebahn.

which the Americans can spy on the town and reassure themselves that it is the same down there as it is on Bald Hill. Herb Gravney sells them ice creams and soft drinks and extra film for their cameras. Here is another who is doing well. He bought the whole model from Mrs Gleason and charges five American dollars admission. Herb is on the council now too. He's doing very well for himself. He sells them the film so they can take photographs of the house and the model people and so they can come down to the town with their special maps and hunt out the real people.

To tell the truth most of us are pretty sick of the game. They come looking for my father and ask him to stare at the gears of Dyer's bicycle. I watch my father cross the street slowly, his head hung low. He doesn't greet the Americans anymore. He doesn't ask them questions about colour television or Washington DC. He kneels on the footpath in front of Dyer's bike. They stand around him. Often they remember the model incorrectly and try to get my father to pose in the wrong way. Originally he argued with them, but now he argues no more. He does what they ask. They push him this way and that and worry about the expression on his face which is no longer what it was.

Then I know they will come to find me. I am next on the map. I am very popular for some reason. They come in search of me and my petrol pump as they have done for four years now. I do not await them eagerly because I

1 **to reassure o.s.:** sich vergewissern.
10 **to hunt out:** aufstöbern, aufspüren.
17 **DC:** Abk. für *District of Columbia.*
20 **to pose:** sich in Positur stellen.
22 f. **this way and that:** hierhin und dorthin.

know, before they reach me, that they will be disappointed.

"But this is not the boy."

"Yes," says Phonsey, "this is him all right." And he gets me to show them my certificate.

They examine the certificate suspiciously, feeling the paper as if it might be a clever forgery. "No," they declare. (Americans are so confident.) "No," they shake their heads, "this is not the real boy. The real boy is younger."

"He's older now. He used to be younger." Phonsey looks weary when he tells them. He can afford to look weary.

The Americans peer at my face closely. "It's a different boy."

But finally they get their cameras out. I stand sullenly and try to look amused as I did once. Gleason saw me looking amused but I can no longer remember how it felt. I was looking at Brian Sparrow. But Brian is also tired. He finds it difficult to do his clownish antics and to the Americans his little act isn't funny. They prefer the model. I watch him sadly, sorry that he must perform for such an unsympathetic audience.

The Americans pay one dollar for the right to take our photographs. Having paid the money they are worried about being cheated. They spend their time being disappointed and I spend my time feeling guilty, that I have somehow let them down by growing older and sadder.

7 **forgery:** Fälschung.
16 **sullenly** (adv.): mürrisch.
21 **act:** ‚Nummer', Darbietung.
23 **unsympathetic:** teilnahmslos.
28 **to let s.o. down:** jdn. enttäuschen.

Murray Bail

The Drover's Wife

The Drover's Wife (1945)

There has perhaps been a mistake – but of no great importance – made in the denomination of this picture. The woman depicted is not "The Drover's Wife". She is

2 **drover:** Viehtreiber.
4 **denomination:** Bezeichnung, Titelgebung.
5 **to depict:** (ab)malen, bildlich darstellen.

my wife. We have not seen each other now . . . it must be getting on thirty years. This portrait was painted shortly after she left – and had joined him. Notice she has very conveniently hidden her wedding hand. It is a canvas 20 × 24 inches, signed 1/r "Russell Drysdale".
I say "shortly after" because she has our small suitcase – Drysdale has made it look like a shopping bag – and she is wearing the sandshoes she normally wore to the beach. Besides, it is dated 1945.
It is Hazel alright.
How much can you tell by a face? That a woman has left a husband and two children? Here, I think the artist has fallen down (though how was he to know?). He has Hazel with a resigned helpless expression – as if it was all my fault. Or, as if she had been a country woman all her ruddy life.
Otherwise the likeness is fair enough.
Hazel was large-boned. Our last argument I remember concerned her weight. She weighed – I have the figures – 12st. 4 ozs. And she wasn't exactly tall. I see that she put it back on almost immediately. It doesn't take long. See her legs.

2 **getting on** (coll.): annähernd.
4 **wedding hand:** etwa: Ringfingerhand.
canvas: Leinwand, Gemälde.
5 **1/r:** wohl Sigle der Signaturplazierung (*r:* Abk. für *right*).
Drysdale: Russell D. (geb. 1912), australischer Maler; bekannt unter anderem für seine Darstellung der Buschlandschaft und ihrer Menschen.
8 **sandshoe:** Strandschuh.
13 **to fall down** (coll.): versagen, enttäuschen.
16 **ruddy:** 1. rotbackig, gesund; 2. (slang) verflixt, verdammt.
18 **large-boned:** grobgliedrig.
20 **12 st. 4 ozs.:** Abk. für *12 stone 4 ounces:* 153 Pfund.
21 **to put on:** (Fett) ansetzen.

She had a small, pretty face, I'll give her that. I was always surprised by her eyes. How solemn they were. The painting shows that. Overall, a gentle face, one that other women liked. How long it must have lasted up in the drought conditions is anybody's guess.

A drover! Why a drover? It has come as a shock to me.

"I am just going round the corner," she wrote, characteristically. It was a piece of butcher's paper left on the table.

Then, and this sounded odd at the time: "Your tea's in the oven. Don't give Trev any carrots."

Now that sounded as if she wouldn't be back, but after puzzling over it, I dismissed it.

And I think that is what hurt me most. No "Dear" at the top, not even "Gordon". No "love" at the bottom. Hazel left without so much as a goodbye. We could have talked it over.

Adelaide is a small town. People soon got to know. They . . . shied away. I was left alone to bring up Trevor and Kay. It took a long time – years – before, if asked, I could say: "She vamoosed. I haven't got a clue to where."

1 **I'll give her that:** Das muß ich ihr lassen.
3 **overall** (adv.): insgesamt.
5 **drought:** Trockenheit, Dürre.
9 **butcher's paper:** Pergamentpapier (zum Einwickeln von Fleischwaren).
14 **to puzzle over s.th.:** sich den Kopf über etwas zerbrechen.
17 f. **to talk s.th. over:** etwas besprechen.
19 **Adelaide:** Hauptstadt des Staates South Australia mit 16 000 Einwohnern im engeren bzw. 800 000 im weiteren Stadtgebiet.
22 **to vamoose** (coll.): verduften, Leine ziehen.
I haven't got a clue (coll.): ich hab keinen Schimmer.

Fancy coming across her in a painting, one reproduced in colour at that. I suppose in a way that makes Hazel famous.

The picture gives little away though. It is the outback – but where exactly? South Australia? It could easily be Queensland, West Australia, the Northern Territory. We don't know. You could never find that spot.

He is bending over (feeding?) the horse, so it is around dusk. This is borne out by the length of Hazel's shadow. It is probably in the region of 5 p.m. Probably still over the hundred mark. What a place to spend the night. The silence would have already begun.

Hazel looks unhappy. I can see she is having second thoughts. Alright, it was soon after she had left me; but she is standing away, in the foreground, as though they're not speaking. See that? Distance = doubts. They've had an argument.

Of course, I want to know all about him. I don't even know his name. In Drysdale's picture he is a silhouette. A completely black figure. He could have been an Aborigine; by the late forties I understand some were employed as drovers.

1 **fancy:** nicht zu fassen, daß . . .
2 **at that:** obendrein.
4 **to give s.th. away:** etwas verraten.
though (adv., coll.): trotzdem, aber, allerdings.
4 f. **outback** (Austral.): Hinterland, Busch.
10 **to bear out:** bestätigen.
12 **hundred mark:** 100° Fahrenheit (37,8° Celsius).
14 f. **to have second thoughts:** sich noch mal (gründlich) Gedanken machen.
22 **Aborigine:** (australischer) Ureinwohner, Eingeborener.

But I rejected that.

I took a magnifying glass. I wanted to see the expression on his face. What colour is his hair? Magnified, he is nothing but brush strokes. A real mystery man.

It is my opinion, however, that he is a small character. See his size in relation to the horse, to the wheels of the cart. Either that, or it is a ruddy big horse.

It begins to fall into place.

I had an argument with our youngest, Kay, the other day. Both she and Trevor sometimes visit me. I might add, she hasn't married and has her mother's general build. She was blaming me, said people said mum was a good sort.

Right. I nodded.

"Then why did she scoot?"

"Your mother," I said thinking quickly, "had a silly streak."

If looks could kill!

I searched around – "She liked to paddle in water!"

Kay gave a nasty laugh, "What? You're the limit. You really are."

Of course, I hadn't explained properly. And I didn't even know then she had gone off with a drover.

2 **magnifying glass:** Vergrößerungsglas, Lupe.
8 **to fall into place:** Zusammenhang ergeben.
12 **build:** Körperbau, Statur.
mum: Mami.
13 **to be a good sort:** als Mensch in Ordnung sein.
15 **to scoot:** abhauen.
16 f. **silly streak:** unbedachtsame Neigung.
20 **nasty:** fies, garstig.
you're the limit (coll.): du bist das letzte.

Hazel was basically shy, even with me: quiet, generally non-committal. At the same time, I can imagine her allowing herself to be painted so soon after running off without leaving even a phone number or forwarding address. It fits. It sounds funny, but it does.

This silly streak. Heavy snow covered Mt. Barker for the first time and we took the Austin up on the Sunday. From a visual point of view it was certainly remarkable. Our gum trees and stringy barks somehow do not go with the white stuff, not even the old Ghost Gum. I mentioned this to Hazel but she just ran into it and began chucking snowballs at me. People were laughing. Then she fell in up to her knees, squawking like a schoolgirl. I didn't mean to speak harshly, but I went up to her, "Come on, don't be stupid. Get up." She went very quiet. She didn't speak for hours.

Kay of course wouldn't remember that.

With the benefit of hindsight, and looking at this portrait by Drysdale, I can see Hazel had a soft side. I think I let her clumsiness get me down. The sight of sweat patches under her arms, for example, somehow put me

2 **non-committal:** zurückhaltend.
4 f. **forwarding address:** Nachsendeadresse.
6 **Mt.:** Abk. für *Mount.*
7 **Austin:** englisches Autofabrikat.
9 **gum tree** (Austral.): Eukalyptus.
stringy: streifig, faserig.
10 **ghost gum** (Austral.): weißstämmiger Eukalyptus.
12 **to chuck:** schmeißen.
13 **to squawk:** kreischen.
18 **hindsight:** späte Einsicht.
20 **clumsiness:** Unbeholfenheit.
to get s.o. down (coll.): jdn. fertigmachen.

in a bad mood. It irritated me the way she chopped wood. I think she enjoyed chopping wood. There was the time I caught her lugging into the house the ice for the ice chest – this is just after the war. The ice man didn't seem to notice; he was following, working out his change. It somehow made her less attractive in my eyes, I don't know why. And then of course she killed that snake down at the beach shack we took one Christmas. I happened to lift the lid of the incinerator – a black brute, its head bashed in. "It was under the house," she explained.

It was a two-roomed shack, bare floorboards. It had a primus stove, and an asbestos toilet down the back. Hazel didn't mind. Quite the contrary; when it came time to leave she was downcast. I had to be at town for work.

The picture reminds me. It was around then Hazel took to wearing just a slip around the house. And bare feet. The dress in the picture looks like a slip. She even used to burn rubbish in it down the back.

I don't know.

"Hello, missus!" I used to say, entering the kitchen. Not

3 **to lug:** (mühsam) zerren, schleppen.
ice chest: Eisschrank.
5 **to work out:** ausrechnen.
8 **shack:** Hütte.
9 **incinerator:** Verbrennungsofen.
10 **to bash in** (coll.): einschlagen, zertrümmern.
12 **floorboards** (pl.): Bretterboden.
13 **primus stove:** Primuskocher (Spirituskocher).
17 f. **to take to doing s.th.:** sich angewöhnen, etwas zu tun.
20 **rubbish:** Abfall, Müll.
22 **missus** (coll.): etwa: Alte (Anrede der ‚besseren Hälfte').

perfect perhaps, especially by today's standards, but that is my way of showing affection. I think Hazel understood. Sometimes I could see she was touched.

I mention that to illustrate our marriage was not all nit-picking and argument. When I realized she had gone I sat for nights in the lounge with the lights out. I am a dentist. You can't have shaking hands and be a dentist. The word passed around. Only now, touch wood, has the practice picked up to any extent.

Does this explain at all why she left?

Not really.

To return to the picture. Drysdale has left out the flies. No doubt he didn't want Hazel waving her hand, or them crawling over her face. Nevertheless, this is a serious omission. It is altering the truth for the sake of a pretty picture, or "composition". I've been up around there – and there are hundreds of flies. Not necessarily germ carriers, "bush flies" I think these are called; and they drive you mad. Hazel of course accepted everything without a song and dance. She didn't mind the heat, or the flies.

It was a camping holiday. We had one of those striped beach tents shaped like a bell. I thought at the time it would prove handy – visible from the air – if we got lost.

4 f. **nit-picking** (coll.): pingelig; Krittelei.
6 **lounge:** Wohnzimmer.
8 **word:** Nachricht.
to pass around: die Runde machen.
touch wood: toi, toi, toi!
9 **to pick up:** sich erholen.
18 **germ carrier:** Bazillenträger.
bush fly: australische Fliegenart.
20 **song and dance** (coll.): Getue.

Now that is a point. Although I will never forget the colours and the assortment of rocks I saw up there I have no desire to return, none. I realized one night. Standing a few yards from the tent, the cavernous sky and the silence all round suddenly made me shudder. I felt lost. It defied logic. And during the day the bush, which is small and prickly, offered no help (I was going to say "sympathy"). It was stinking hot.

Yet Hazel was in her element, so much so she seemed to take no interest in the surroundings. She acted as if she were part of it. I felt ourselves moving apart, as if I didn't belong there, especially with her. I felt left out. My mistake was to believe it was a passing phase, almost a form of indolence on her part.

An unfortunate incident didn't help. We were looking for a camp site. "Not yet. No, not there," I kept saying – mainly to myself, for Hazel let me go on, barely saying a word. At last I found a spot. A tree showed in the dark. We bedded down. Past midnight we were woken by a terrifying noise and lights. The children all began to cry. I had pitched camp alongside the Adelaide–Port Augusta railway line.

Twenty or thirty miles north of Port Augusta I turned back. I had to. We seemed to be losing our senses. We

2 **assortment:** Anordnung.
4 **cavernous:** höhlenartig.
7 **prickly:** stachelig, dornig.
8 **stinking** (slang): widerlich.
9 **so much so:** so sehr, daß . . .
14 **indolence:** Trägheit, Lässigkeit.
19 **to bed down:** sich (behelfsmäßig) betten, einnisten.
21 **to pitch camp:** das Lager errichten, Zelt aufschlagen.
alongside: (dicht) neben.

actually met a drover somewhere around there. He was off on the side making tea. When I asked where were his sheep, or the cattle, he gave a wave of his hand. For some reason this amused Hazel. She squatted down. I can still see her expression, silly girl.

The man didn't say much. He did offer tea though.

"Come on," said Hazel, smiling up at me.

Hazel and her silly streak – she knew I wanted to get back. The drover, a diplomat, poked at the fire with a stick.

I said:

"You can if you want. I'll be in the car."

That is all.

I recall the drover as a thin head in a khaki hat, not talkative, with dusty boots. He is indistinct. Is it him? I don't know. Hazel – it is Hazel and the rotten landscape that dominate everything.

4 **to squat down:** sich hinhocken.
9 **to poke:** schüren, stochern.
14 **to recall s.o.:** sich an jdn. erinnern.
15 **talkative:** gesprächig.
16 **rotten:** verdorben, verkommen, mies.

Fay Zwicky

Hostages

I think I began to hate when I was twelve. Consciously, I mean. The war was then in its fourth year, there was no chocolate and my father was still away in Borneo. I barely knew him. Till then I had learnt to admire what my mother believed to be admirable. Striving to please with ascetic rigour, I practised scales and read Greek myths. Morality hinged on hours of piano practices achieved or neglected. I knew no evil. The uncommon neutrality of my existence as a musical child in wartime was secured in a world neither good nor malevolent. My place among men was given. Did I have feelings? I was not ready to admit them for there seemed to be rules governing their revelation which I either could not or would not grasp. Nameless, passionless, and without daring I repressed deepest candour. But *tout comprendre c'est tout pardonner*; what was once self-indul-

2 **hostage:** Geisel.
8 **ascetic:** asketisch, enthaltsam.
scale: Tonleiter.
9 **to hinge on s.th.:** von etwas abhängen, sich um etwas drehen.
12 **malevolent:** böswillig.
17 **to repress:** unterdrücken.
candour: Offenheit.
17 f. **Tout comprendre c'est tout pardonner** (Fr.): Alles verstehen heißt alles verzeihen (geflügeltes Wort nach Madame de Staëls *Corinne*, 1807).
18 f. **self-indulgence:** Sich-Gehenlassen.

gence is now permissible revelation. Why, then, should shame crimp the edge of my reflection so many years after the event?

Sophie Lindauer-Grünberg, German refugee, piano teacher, used to visit our house once a week. Poor fat sentimental Sophie, grateful recipient of my mother's pity. I was to be her first Australian pupil.

"But why me?"

"Because she needs help. She was nothing and you, thank God, have everything. She's been a very fine musician in her own country. You have to understand that this is someone who has lost everything. Yes, you can roll your eyes. *Everything*, I said. Something I hope, please God, that will never happen to you. So you'll be nice to her and pay attention to what she says. I've told Mr Grover he lives too far away for me to go on taking you to lessons twice a week."

Suddenly dull and bumbling Mr Grover in his music room smelling of tobacco and hair oil seemed like my last contact with the outside world. I was to be corralled into the tight, airless circle of maternal philanthropy.

1 **permissible:** statthaft.
2 **to crimp** (slang): stören, behindern.
edge: Schärfe.
4 **refugee:** Flüchtling.
6 **recipient:** Empfänger(in).
14 **please God:** so Gott will.
18 **bumbling:** stümperhaft.
20 **to corral:** einpferchen.
21 **airless:** stickig.
maternal: mütterlich.
philanthropy: Menschenliebe.

The day of my first lesson a hot north wind was tearing at the huge gum in front of the house. Blinds and curtains were drawn against the promised heat. The house stood girded like an island under siege. My younger brother and sister had gone swimming. I watched them go, screwing up my eyes with the beginnings of a headache, envying their laughter and the way they tore sprigs off the lantana plants lining the driveway. I awaited my teacher, a recalcitrant hostage. The rooms were generous and high-ceilinged but I prowled about, tight-lipped, seeking yet more room. A deep nerve of anger throbbed in me and I prayed that she would not come. But she came. Slowly up the brick path in the heat. I watched her from the window, measuring her heavy step with my uneasy breath. Then my mother's voice greeting her in the hallway, high-pitched and over-articulated as if her listener were deaf, a standard affectation of hers with foreign visitors. "Terrible day ... trouble finding the house ... Helen looking forward so much ..." I ran to the bathroom and turned on the tap hard. I just let

2 **gum** (*tree*) (Austral.): Eukalyptus.
4 **to gird:** umgeben, umschließen.
6 **to screw up one's eyes:** die Augen zusammenkneifen, verdrehen.
8 **sprig:** Schößling.
lantana: Wandelröschen.
to line: (Weg) säumen.
driveway: Einfahrt.
9 **recalcitrant:** widerspenstig, aufsässig.
10 **to prowl about:** herumstreichen, -streifen.
10 f. **tight-lipped:** verkniffen.
12 **to throb:** beben, zittern.
16 **hallway:** Eingangshalle.
high-pitched: in hoher Stimmlage.
over-articulated: mit überdeutlicher Aussprache.

it run, catching sight of my face in the mirror above the basin.

Could I be called pretty? Brown hair hanging long on either side of high cheekbones, the hint of a powerful nose to come, a chin too long, cold grey eyes, wide mouth, fresh colour. No, not pretty. No heroine either. A wave of self-pity compensated me for what I saw and tears filled my eyes. Why me? Because she has to have pupils. Am I such a prize? No, but a Jew who has everything. "Be thankful you were born in this wonderful country." My mother's voice sounded loud in my ears. "They're making them into lamp shades over there." I had laughed, but shrank from the grotesque absurdity of the statement. Why the dramatics? All I remember is the enveloping anger directed at everything my life had been and was. I wanted to be left alone but didn't know how or where to begin. "She has lost her whole family. Taken away and shot before her eyes . . ." So? Now she has me.

My mother and Miss Grünberg were talking about me as I stood in the doorway. My own hands were clammy as I moved forward to the outstretched, unfamiliar gesture. Hers were small, fat and very white, surprisingly small for such a tall, heavily built woman, like soft snuggling grubs. She herself looked like some swollen, pale grub smiling widely and kindly, a spinster of nearly

12 **lamp shade:** Lampenschirm.
14 **dramatics** (pl.): Theatralik.
15 **to envelop:** um-, einhüllen.
21 **clammy:** feuchtkalt.
25 **to snuggle:** sich anschmiegen.
grub: Raupe, Larve.
26 **spinster:** alte Jungfer.

sixty. Her little eyes gleamed through thick, round spectacles. On the skin beneath her eyes tiny bluish vessels spread their nets.

"So here is *unsere liebe Helene*!"

I raised my eyebrows insolently, as the girls did at school, after one of my ill-judged observations. It was essential to the code governing the treatment of victims. But this time I had the upper hand and didn't know how to handle my advantage. The cobbles of Cologne and Cracow rang hollow under my boots. The light from the pink shaded lamp fell on my new teacher. The wind blew in sharp gusts outside.

"Helen, this is Miss Grünberg." My mother with a sharp look in my direction. "I've been telling her about the work you've done so far with Mr Grover. Miss Grünberg would like you to have another book of studies."

"Perhaps you will play *ein Stück* for me. Liszt perhaps?" She nodded ponderously at our Bechstein grand that suddenly took on the semblance of some monstrous piece of abstract statuary, out of all proportion to the scale of the room.

"Lord, no. I've never done him." I fell into uncharacter-

6 **ill-judged:** unbedacht.
7 **code:** Kodex, Normen, Gesetze.
9 **cobbles** (pl.): Kopfsteinpflaster.
12 **gust:** Bö.
16 f. **book of studies:** hier: Etüdenheft.
19 **ponderously** (adv.): gewichtig, schwerfällig.
grand: Flügel (Klavier).
20 **to take on the semblance:** die Gestalt annehmen.
21 **statuary:** Bildhauerei.
out of all proportion to: in keinem Verhältnis zu.
23 **Lord:** du lieber Gott!

istic breeziness. "I'm not really in practice. Hardly anything going at the moment and I'm pretty stale on the stuff Grover had me on for the exams." Deliberately fast, consciously idiomatic, enjoying, yes *enjoying* the strain of comprehension on my victim's round, perpetually smiling face.

"You can *still* play those Debussy *Arabesques*," said my mother, her neck flushed. "I put the music on the piano," and she gave me yet another warning look.

I opened the lid noisily and sat down with elaborate movements, shifting the metronome a few inches to the right, altering the position of the stand, bending to examine my feet fumbling between the pedals. The *Arabesques* moved perfunctorily. I kept my face impassive, looked rigidly ahead at the music which I didn't see. Even during the section I liked in the second piece, a part where normally I would lean back a little and smile. I had begun to learn how not to please. But the process of self-annihilation involved the destruction of others. *Tout pardonner* did I say?

Miss Grünberg arranged with my mother to return the following week at the same time.

"Why are you behaving like this?" asked my mother, red and angry with me after she had left in a taxi.

1 **breeziness:** Forschheit.
1 f. **hardly anything going** (coll.): (es) läuft kaum was.
2 **to be stale on s.th.:** von etwas angeödet sein.
3 **to have s.o. on s.th.:** jdn. auf etwas ansetzen.
12 **stand:** (Noten-)Ständer.
13 **to fumble:** umhertappen.
14 **perfunctorily** (adv.): mechanisch.
impassive: teilnahmslos.
19 **self-annihilation:** Selbstzerstörung.

The young blond driver had tapped his foot noisily on the brick path as Miss Grünberg profusely repeated her gratitude to my mother for the privilege of teaching her talented daughter. Moving rapidly away from them I conversed with him, broadening my vowels like sharks' teeth on the subject of the noon temperature. I was desperate that the coveted outside world and its tranquil normality should recognize that I was in no way linked with the heavy foreign accent involved in demonstrative leave-taking on our front lawn.

"Behaving like what?"

"You know what I mean. You behaved abominably to that poor woman."

"I played for her, didn't I?" She came closer to me with a vengeful mouth.

"You could call it that. I don't know what's got into you lately. You used to be such a good child. Now you know the answers to everything. A walking miracle! What terrible things have we done, your father and I, that you should behave like a pig to a woman like that? We've given you everything. *Everything*! And because I'm good to an unfortunate refugee who needs help wher-

1 **to tap one's foot:** mit dem Fuß (auf den Boden) klopfen.
2 **profusely** (adv.): überschwenglich.
6 **shark:** Hai(fisch).
7 **to covet:** begehren.
8 **tranquil:** ruhig, friedlich.
10 **demonstrative:** auffällig, betont.
leave-taking: Verabschiedung.
13 **abominably** (adv.): abscheulich.
16 **vengeful:** rachsüchtig.
17 **what's got into you:** was in dich gefahren ist.
19 **walking:** wandelnd, leibhaftig.

ever she can find it, you have to behave like that! I'm sorry for you, *really* sorry for you!"

"Spare your sympathy for the poor reffoes!" The taxi driver's word burst savagely out of my mouth. She flew at me and slapped me across the face with her outstretched hand.

"One thing I do know," she was trembling with rage, "the one thing I'm sure of is that I've been too good to you. We've given you too much. You're spoilt rotten! And *one* day, my girl, one day you too may be old and unwanted and . . ."

"A lampshade perhaps? So what." I shook with guilt and fear at the enormity of what I'd said, terrified of the holocaust I'd shaken loose and my mother's twisted mouth.

But the revolution didn't get under way, either that day or that year. The heroine lacked (should one say it?) courage. Sealed trains are more comforting than the unknown wastes of the steppes. The following week Miss Grünberg toiled up our front path and I sat down to the new course of Moscheles studies and a movement of a Mozart concerto. *Her* music. Scored heavily in red pencil, the loved and hated language dotted with emo-

3 **reffo** (Austral., coll.): Flüchtling (aus Europa).
5 **to slap:** schlagen.
9 **spoilt rotten** (coll.): etwa: verwöhnt bis zum Geht-nicht-mehr.
14 **holocaust:** Vernichtung (Wortspiel mit *the Holocaust* ›die Judenvernichtung‹).
16 **to get under way:** in Gang kommen.
21 **Moscheles:** Ignaz M. (1794–1870), deutscher Pianist und Komponist; ab 1846 Leiter der Klavierausbildung am Leipziger Konservatorium. **movement:** (musikalischer) Satz.
22 **to score:** markieren.

tional exclamation marks. Her life's work put out for my ruthless inspection. She moved her chair closer to my stool to alter the position of my right hand. "Finger *rund, Kleine*, always *rund*. Hold always the wrist supple, *liebe Helene*." I shrank from the alien endearment and her sour breath but curved my fingers, tight and deliberate. Her smell hung over me, a static haze in the dry air. Musty, pungent and stale, the last faint reminder of an airless Munich apartment house. Her dress, a cheap silky fabric, rustled when she moved her heavy body. Breathing laboriously she tried to explain to me what I should do with the Mozart. She couldn't get used to the heat of the new country and was beginning to find walking difficult. But I didn't practise between her visits and gave only spasmodic attention to her gentle directions. I was shutting myself off from words and from music, beginning a long course in alienation. I seldom looked my mother in the eye in those days. I quarrelled bitterly with my sister, ignored my brother.

2 **ruthless:** unbarmherzig, rücksichtslos.
5 **supple:** biegsam, geschmeidig.
alien: fremdartig.
5 f. **endearment:** Zuneigung, Zärtlichkeit.
7 **static:** statisch, gleichbleibend.
8 **haze:** Dunst(schleier).
musty: muffig, modrig.
pungent: stechend, beißend.
stale: schal, abgestanden.
10 **silky fabric:** seidiger Stoff.
11 **laboriously** (adv.): mühsam, schwer.
15 **spasmodic:** vereinzelt, sporadisch.
16 f. **to shut o.s. off s.th.:** sich gegen etwas sperren.
18 **alienation:** Entfremdung.

About six months after my lessons with Miss Grünberg started I was not much further advanced. I spent a lot of time reading in my room or just looking out of the window at the garden which was now bare. Squalls lashed the gum tree and drove the leaves from the weeping elm skittering across the grass. Miss Grünberg now had several pupils amongst the children of the Jewish community and even one or two gentiles from the neighbouring school. She lived in a very poorly furnished flat in a rundown outer suburb. She still travelled to her pupils' homes. Her breathing had become very short in the last few weeks. Inattentive and isolated as I was, I had noticed that she was even paler than usual.

My mother one day told me with some rancour how well the Lapin girl was doing with the piano. "She never had your talent but what a worker! She's going to give a recital in the Assembly Hall next month." I merely shrugged. The boots of the conqueror were no picnic. She was welcome to them. "And while I'm about it, I've decided to tell Miss Grünberg not to come any more. I don't feel there's much point as you seem quite determined to do as little with music as possible. I've done all *I* can. At least she's on her feet now." On her feet! Oh

4 **squall:** Sturmbö.
5 **to lash:** peitschen.
6 **weeping elm:** Trauerulme.
to skitter: entlangstreifen, dahinjagen.
8 **gentile:** Nicht-Jude.
10 **rundown:** heruntergekommen, baufällig.
15 **rancour:** Erbitterung, Groll.
17 f. **to give a recital:** vorspielen, ein Konzert geben.
24 **to be on one's feet:** (fig.) (wieder) auf den Beinen sein, Fuß fassen.

God! But I replied, "That's all right with me", in as neutral a voice as I could summon.
But that night I ground my face into the covers of my bed, no longer a place of warmth and security but a burial trench. At the mercy of my dreams appeared Sophie Lindauer-Grünberg, pale as brick dust. Her face wasting, crumbling to ash, blasted by the force of my terrible youth. And, waking in fright, I mourned for the first time my innocent victim and our shared fate.

1 **that's all right with me:** das soll mir recht sein.
2 **to summon:** aufbringen, -bieten.
3 **to grind:** reiben, quetschen.
5 **trench:** Graben.
(*to be*) **at the mercy of s.th.:** etwas preisgegeben, ausgeliefert sein.
7 **to blast:** verdorren lassen, vernichten.

David Malouf

The Only Speaker of His Tongue

He has already been pointed out to me: a flabby, thickset man of fifty-five or sixty, very black, working alongside the others and in no way different from them – or so it seems. When they work he swings his pick with the same rhythm. When they pause he squats and rolls a cigarette, running his tongue along the edge of the paper while his eyes, under the stained hat, observe the straight line of the horizon; then he sets it between his lips, cups flame, draws in, and blows out smoke like all the rest.

Wears moleskins looped low under his belly and a flannel vest. Sits at smoko on one heel and sips tea from an enamel mug. Spits, and his spit hisses on stone. Then rises, spits in his palm and takes up the pick. They are

3 **to point s.o. out:** auf jdn. hinweisen, aufmerksam machen.
flabby: schlaff, schlapp.
3 f. **thickset:** untersetzt, stämmig.
4 f. **alongside:** Seite an Seite mit, neben.
6 **pick:** Spitzhacke.
7 **to squat:** (sich) hocken.
11 **to cup flame:** mit hohler Hand anzünden.
13 **moleskins** (pl.): Hose aus Moleskin (Baumwollgewebe).
to loop: (mit einer Schleife) zusammen-, festbinden.
13 f. **flannel vest:** Flanellweste.
14 **smoko** (Austral., coll.): Paffpause, kurze Arbeitspause.
to sip: schlürfen, in kleinen Schlucken trinken.
15 **enamel mug:** Emailbecher.

digging holes for fencing-posts at the edge of the plain. When called he answers immediately, "Here, boss," and then, when he has approached, "Yes boss, you wanna see me?" I am presented and he seems amused, as if I were some queer northern bird he had heard about but never till now believed in, a sort of crane perhaps, with my grey frock-coat and legs too spindly in their yellow trousers; an odd, angular fellow with yellow-grey side-whiskers, half spectacles and a cold-sore on his lip. So we stand face to face.

He is, they tell me, the one surviving speaker of his tongue. Half a century back, when he was a boy, the last of his people were massacred. The language, one of hundreds (why make a fuss?) died with them. Only not quite. For all his lifetime this man has spoken it, if only to himself. The words, the great system of sound and silence (for all languages, even the simplest, are a great and complex system) are locked up now in his heavy skull, behind the folds of the black brow (hence my scholarly interest), in the mouth with its stained teeth and fat, rather pink tongue. It is alive still in the man's silence, a whole alternative universe, since the world as we know it is in the last resort the words through which

1 **fencing-post:** Zaunpfahl, -pfosten.
3 **wanna:** *want to.*
6 **crane:** Kranich.
7 **frock-coat:** Gehrock.
spindly: spindeldürr.
8 **angular:** steif, linkisch.
8 f. **side-whiskers** (pl.): Backenbart.
9 **half spectacles** (pl.): Brille mit halben Gläsern.
cold-sore: Herpes (Bläschenausschlag).
14 **why make a fuss:** warum sich aufregen?
20 **scholarly:** wissenschaftlich.
23 **in the last resort:** zu guter Letzt.

we imagine and name it; and when he narrows his eyes, and grins and says "Yes, boss, you wanna see me?", it is not breathed out.

I am (you may know my name) a lexicographer. I come to these shores from far off, out of curiosity, a mere tourist, but in my own land I too am the keeper of something: of the great book of words of my tongue. No, not mine, my people's, which they have made over centuries, up there in our part of the world, and in which, if you have an ear for these things and a nose for the particular fragrance of a landscape, you may glimpse forests, lakes, great snow-peaks that hang over our land like the wings of birds. It is all there in our mouths. In the odd names of our villages, in the pet-names we give to pigs or cows, and to our children too when they are young, Little Bean, Pretty Cowslip; in the nonsense rhymes in which so much simple wisdom is contained (not by accident, the language itself discovers these truths), or in the way, when two consonants catch up a repeated sound, a new thought goes flashing from one side to another of your head.

All this is mystery. It is a mystery of the deep past, but also of now. We recapture on our tongue, when we first grasp the sound and make it, the same word in the mouths of our long dead fathers, whose blood we move in and whose blood still moves in us. Language *is* that blood. It is the sun taken up where it shares out heat and

3 **to breathe out:** (fig.) ausatmen, verlautbaren.
4 **lexicographer:** Lexikograph, Wörterbuchverfasser.
11 **fragrance:** Duft.
16 **cowslip:** Schlüsselblume.
19 **to catch up:** aufhalten, unterbrechen.
23 **to recapture:** (fig.) wieder einfangen, wieder lebendig werden lassen.
27 **to share out:** austeilen.

light to the surface of each thing and made whole, hot, round again. *Solen*, we say, and the sun stamps once on the plain and pushes up in its great hot body, trailing streams of breath.

O holiest of all holy things! – it is a stooped blond crane that tells you this, with yellow side-whiskers and the grey frock-coat and trousers of his century – since we touch here on beginnings, go deep down under Now to the remotest dark, far back in each ordinary moment of our speaking, even in gossip and the rigmarole of love words and children's games, into the lives of our fathers, to share with them the single instant of all our seeing and making, all our long history of doing and being. When I think of my tongue being no longer alive in the mouths of men a chill goes over me that is deeper than my own death, since it is the gathered death of all my kind. It is black night descending once and forever on all that world of forests, lakes, snow-peaks, great birds' wings; on little fishing sloops, on foxes nosing their way into a coop, on the piles of logs that make bonfires, and the heels of the young girls leaping over them, on sewing-needles, milk pails, axes, on gingerbread moulds made out of good birchwood, on fiddles, school

2 **solen** (Norw.): die Sonne.
3 **to trail:** hinter sich herziehen.
10 **rigmarole:** sinnloses Geplapper.
17 **kind:** Geschlecht.
19 **sloop:** Schaluppe.
to nose: wittern, erspüren.
20 **coop:** Hühnerstall.
bonfire: Freudenfeuer.
22 **gingerbread:** Pfefferkuchen.
23 **mould:** Backform.
fiddle: Fiedel.

slates, spinning-tops – my breath catches, my heart jumps. O the holy dread of it! Of having under your tongue the first and last words of all those generations down there in your blood, down there in the earth, for whom these syllables were the magic once for calling the whole of creation to come striding, swaying, singing towards them. I look at this old fellow and my heart stops, I do not know what to say to him.

I am curious, of course – what else does it mean to be a scholar but to be curious and to have a passion for the preserving of things? I would like to have him speak a word or two in his own tongue. But the desire is frivolous, I am ashamed to ask. And in what language would I do it? This foreign one? Which I speak out of politeness because I am a visitor here, and speak well because I have learned it, and he because it is the only one he can share now with his contemporaries, with those who fill the days with him – the language (he appears to know only a handful of words) of those who feed, clothe, employ him, and whose great energy, and a certain gift for changing and doing things, has set all this land under another tongue. For the land too is in another language now. All its capes and valleys have new names; so do its creatures – even the insects that make their own skirling, racketing sound under stones. The first landscape here is dead. It dies in this man's eyes as his tongue licks

1 **slate:** Schiefertafel.
spinning-top: Kreisel.
to catch: anhalten, stocken (Atem).
12 f. **frivolous:** leichtfertig.
17 **contemporary:** Zeitgenosse.
24 f. **to skirl:** (schrill) pfeifen.
25 **to racket:** lärmen.

the edge of the horizon, before it has quite dried up in his mouth. There is a new one now that others are making.

So. It is because I am a famous visitor, a scholarly freak from another continent, that we have been brought together. We have nothing to say to one another. I come to the fire where he sits with the rest of the men and accept a mug of their sweet scalding tea. I squat with difficulty in my yellow trousers. We nod to one another. He regards me with curiosity, with a kind of shy amusement, and sees what? Not fir forests, surely, for which he can have neither picture nor word, or lakes, snow-peaks, a white bird's wing. The sun perhaps, our northern one, making a long path back into the dark, and the print of our feet, black tracks upon it.

Nothing is said. The men are constrained by the presence of a stranger, but also perhaps by the presence of the boss. They make only the most rudimentary attempts at talk: slow monosyllabic remarks, half-swallowed with the tea. The thread of community here is strung with a few shy words and expletives – grunts, caws, soft bursts of laughter that go back before syntax; the man no more talkative than the rest, but a presence just the same.

4 **freak:** verrückter Kerl, Spinner.
8 **scalding:** brühend heiß.
16 **constrained:** gezwungen, verkrampft, befangen.
18 **rudimentary:** rudimentär, elementar.
19 **monosyllabic:** einsilbig.
21 **expletive:** Füllwort, Fluch(-wort).
grunt: Grunzer.
22 **caw:** Krächzer.
23 **talkative:** gesprächig.
presence: hier: spürbare Anwesenheit.

I feel his silence. He sits here, solid, black, sipping his tea and flicking away with his left hand at a fly that returns again and again to a spot beside his mouth; looks up so level, so much on the horizontal, under the brim of his hat.

Things centre themselves upon him – that is what I feel, it is eerie – as on the one and only repository of a name they will lose if he is no longer there to keep it in mind. He holds thus, on a loose thread, the whole circle of shabby-looking trees, the bushes with their hidden life, the infinitesimal coming and going among grassroots or on ant-trails between stones, the minds of small native creatures that come creeping to the edge of the scene and look in at us from their other lives. He gives no sign of being special. When their smoking time is up, he rises with the rest, stretches a little, spits in the palm of his hand, and goes silently to his work.

"Yes boss, you wanna see me" – neither a statement nor a question, the only words I have heard him speak . . .

I must confess it. He has given me a fright. Perhaps it is only that I am cut off here from the use of my own tongue (though I have never felt such a thing on previous travels, in France, Greece, Egypt), but I find it

2 **to flick away at s.th.:** etwas mit Handbewegungen verscheuchen.
4 **brim:** Krempe.
6 **to centre:** sich richten, konzentrieren.
7 **eerie:** unheimlich.
repository: Behältnis, Fundgrube.
10 **shabby-looking:** von heruntergekommenem Aussehen.
11 **infinitesimal:** verschwindend klein.
14 **to look in:** einen Einblick gewinnen.
21 **to give s.o. a fright:** jdn. in Schrecken versetzen.

necessary, in the privacy of my little room with its marble-topped washbasin and commodious jug and basin, and the engraving of Naomi bidding farewell to Ruth – I find it necessary, as I pace up and down on the scrubbed boards in the heat of a long December night, to go over certain words as if it were only my voice naming them in the dark that kept the loved objects solid and touchable in the light up there, on the top side of the world. (Goodness knows what sort of spells my hostess thinks I am making, or the children, who see me already as a spook, a half-comic, half-sinister wizard of the north.)

So I say softly as I curl up with the sheet over my head, or walk up and down, or stand at the window a moment before this plain that burns even at midnight: *rogn, valnøtt, spiseskje, hakke, vinglass, lysestake, krabbe, kjegle . . .*

2 **marble-topped:** mit Marmorplatte.
commodious: zweckdienlich, praktisch.
3 **engraving:** (Kupfer-)Stich.
3 f. **Naomi bidding farewell to Ruth:** Episode im Buch Ruth 1 des A.T.
5 **to scrub:** schrubben, scheuern.
9 **spell:** Zauberspruch.
11 **spook:** Spukgestalt.
half-sinister: halb unheilvoll, finster.
wizard: Magier.
13 **to curl up:** sich kuscheln, gemütlich zusammenrollen.
15 f. **rogn . . . kjegle** (Norw.): (Fisch-)Rogen; Walnuß; Eßlöffel; Hacke; Weinglas; (Kerzen-)Leuchter; Krabbe; Kegel.

Archie Weller

Pension Day

All day the old black man sits, away from everyone else. He wears the same old black coat every day. Once it had silver buttons and a silk collar and was worn in the best society – with speeches, silver and champagne.
Now it has no buttons and sits upon the hunched back of the leader of the redback people. The people who hug the dark corners and scuttle hideously from rusted hiding place to rusted hiding place. Away from the pale blue eyes that are like the sun, burning everything away so all is stark and straight and true, and there are no cool secrets left.
No one wants to know any of the secrets, anyway.
He sits in the park, the old man, like one of the war cannons that guard the perimeter and stick their long green noses out threateningly at the cars that swish by, not even knowing they are there. Today's children leap and

2 **pension day:** Rentengeldtag (Wochentag der Ausszahlung).
7 **to hunch:** sich krümmen, beugen.
8 **redback people** (Austral.): Stamm der Aborigines (australische Ureinwohner).
to hug s.th.: sich dicht an etwas halten.
9 **to scuttle:** flitzen.
hideously (adv.): scheußlich.
12 **stark** (fig.): nackt, bloß.
16 **perimeter:** Umkreis, Umgrenzung.
17 **to swish by:** vorbeisausen.

laugh over silent steel to further demolish yesterday's pride.

There is no room for yesterday's people.

He is a Wongi from out near Laverton, and he can hardly speak English. When he first came to Perth many years ago, he huddled in the back of the police Land Rover and moaned in terror as the ground swept away before him and trees and rocks and mountains and towns and his whole universe disappeared in a blur. Had it not been for the handcuffs around his great wrists, he would have leaped out the door and ended it all then.

The white men had torn him away from his red land's breast for a crime he could not understand.

A life for a life. That was how the law had worked since before everything. The law was the law.

Yet the Land Rover lurched out to the camp and the three policemen had sprung upon him, taking him by surprise as he sat, singing softly, by his campfire.

The dogs had barked, the children screamed, his young girl-woman, already full with child-spirit, cried, and he had fought with all his strength.

1 **to demolish:** niederreißen, zerstören.

4 **Wongi** (Austral.): speziell: westaustralischer Aborigine-Stamm; allg.: Vollblut-Aborigine.
Laverton: etwa 1000 km nordöstlich von Perth (der Hauptstadt von Western Australia) gelegener Ort.

6 **to huddle:** sich (zusammen)kauern.

10 **blur:** wirrer Nebel, Schleier.
handcuffs: Handschellen.

13 **red land:** weithin roterdiges Landesinnere Australiens.

17 **to lurch:** schlingern, ruckeln.

21 **child-spirit** (Austral.): Kind-Geist (der im Aborigine-Glauben den zunächst nur physisch gezeugten Fötus spirituell belebt).

The old men had watched with silent, all-knowing eyes as he was overpowered and two policemen held him while the sergeant clipped on the handcuffs triumphantly.

He took one last look at his night-blackened land and the black shut faces in the red firelight. Rubbed red dust over his horny feet before being pushed gently into the hard, hot Land Rover. A tear slid out of his frightened, puzzled eyes before he closed his mind and hunched into himself.

He was only about eighteen then and although he wore a pair of scruffed grubby moleskins (and an army slouch hat he kept for special occasions) he had only seen white men six times in his whole life.

So that was that.

When he came out of jail seven years later, he was still strong and proud. No one had been able to touch him in there. He had worked all day and at night he had willed himself out over the walls back to his country.

Red dust and thin mulga bushes and glittering seas of broken glass from the miners' camps. Yellow-sided holes many metres deep. Black open mouths gulping in the hot air and holding white man secrets and dreams.

2 **to overpower:** überwältigen.
3 **to clip on:** befestigen, anlegen.
9 **to close one's mind:** (fig.) sich verschließen, abschalten.
9 f. **to hunch into o.s.:** sich zusammenkauern.
12 **scruffed** (coll.): ramponiert.
grubby: schmuddelig.
moleskins (pl.): Hose aus Moleskin (Baumwollgewebe).
12 f. **slouch hat:** Schlapphut.
20 **mulga:** australische Akazienart.
22 **to gulp in:** herunterschlucken, -schlingen.

Just the place to hide a body snapped in two by powerful hands.

He could never go home again. He would have been killed out at the gabbling, dusty camp, if not by the relatives of his victim, certainly by the new husband to whom the elders would long ago have given his woman.

So he had no country. He had no home. He decided to learn more about the white man's ways that had so awed him.

But what could *he* do? A young man with big muscles, a quick temper, not much knowledge of English – and a black skin? After a few fights in a few country towns, he settled down, working for a produce store deep down south and doing some shearing on the side.

He loved that town. His boss was a good man who protected the angry giant from the taunts that sometimes whipped through the air. It was his boss, too, who found him a good half-caste girl from the nearby mission.

They called him "Jackie Snow" and the name stuck: Snowy Jackson, the straight-shouldered, black colossus

1 **to snap in two:** in zwei Teile brechen.
4 **to gabble:** schwatzen, plappern.
12 **quick temper:** hitziges, aufbrausendes Temperament.
14 **produce store** (Austral.): Warenladen.
15 **shearing:** Schafschur.
on the side: nebenbei.
17 **taunt:** Schmähung.
18 **to whip:** geißeln.
19 **half-caste:** Mischling, Halbblut.
20 **Jackie Snow:** Anspielung auf Jacky Howe (1855–1932), mehrfacher Meister bei den australischen Schafschurwettkämpfen (*Jackie* [Austral., slang]: Aborigine).
to stick: (fig.) hängenbleiben.

among his brown, sharper brethren. There was no love lost between the full-blood and the half-castes. They jeered at the way he worked so hard and refused to share his money around. But they were afraid of his physical and spiritual powers. For wasn't he one from the shimmering emptiness of the desert, a man who came with laws and secrets the brown staggering people had lost or only half-remembered?

He did not tell them that he had lost those, too.

At the produce store he was always cheerful and he kept out of trouble. His educated half-caste wife taught him a little more English, but he never learned how to read or write.

They got their citizenship rights and a little house, just off the track to the town's reserve. Every evening, especially in winter, his wife read the Bible and he stared into the searing heart of the fire with thoughtful, quiet eyes, and tried to remember before.

But this was his life now.

At shearing time they put him on the yard work. He loved to stride through the greasy, grey sea, shouting in his own language and clapping his huge hands so they sounded like the echoes from the thunder in the sky

1 **sharp:** gewitzt, pfiffig.
brethren: (Glaubens-, Stammes-)Brüder.
2 **to lose:** hier: vergeuden.
3 **to jeer at s.th.:** etwas verhöhnen, über etwas spotten.
10 f. **to keep out of trouble:** keine Scherereien machen.
14 **citizenship rights:** Bürgerrechte (den Aborigines per Verfassungsänderung erst 1967 zuerkannt).
15 **reserve:** Reservat.
17 **to sear:** versengen.
20 **to put s.o. on s.th.:** jdn. auf etwas ansetzen, mit etwas betrauen.
21 **greasy:** schmierig.

above. He would fling his head back and flare his nostrils like a wild black horse, and the sheep would pour into the darkened tin woolshed with a furious clicketty-clatter on the wooden grating floor. He felt like a king then, a leader of the people.

The other shearers respected Snowy Jackson for his size and strength. Who else could lift a bleating struggling sheep up above his head and still flash the huge white grin he wore (like his slouch hat for special occasions).

But he used to grow angry sometimes, and picking the stupid sheep up by their shaggy necks he would hurl them into the yard, sometimes killing them.

Then they put him on the shearing team alongside all the white men. He was at last one of them, and he took great pride in his new position. After he got over his first hesitation at the whining shears, he became quite skilled at peeling off the curly wool so it lay, wrinkled and ready, around his feet. Each bald, skinny, white sheep

1 f. **to flare one's nostrils:** die Nüstern blähen.
3 **woolshed** (Austral.): Wollschuppen (zur Schafschur, Wollbearbeitung usw.)
4 **clicketty-clatter:** Klippergeklapper.
grating: Gitter(werk).
7 **to bleat:** blöken.
8 **to flash:** aufblitzen lassen.
12 **shaggy:** zottig.
14 **alongside:** Seite an Seite mit, neben.
17 **to whine:** heulen, jaulen; wimmern.
shears (pl.): (große) Schere.
18 **to peel off:** abstreifen.
curly: lockig, gekräuselt.
wrinkled: kraus.
19 **bald:** kahl.
skinny: mager.

that he pushed down the chute was a new piece of juicy fruit for him to chew on, until his belly was full of white man respect.

Every night when he went home, he would try to explain his joyful day to his little wife, just as once, as a successful hunter, he had recounted his stories to his young woman way away up in the red, swirling Dreaming. But he could not tell the half-caste anything and, after a while, he would stop his broken, happy mumbling and stare into his fire. He would smile softly at things that had happened that day, while the stories came out of his eyes and nestled amongst the coals so he could see them again the next night.

Dreams, dreams.

One year, his young wife died giving birth to her fourth child.

All her relatives came down for the funeral. They sat around talking and remembering, and catching up on the news. Then they all got back in their old cars and trucks and left.

He just has the rain now, turning the sky grey and the world cold. He used to love the rain. He could stand for hours in the soft drizzle and let all the secrets from the

1 **chute:** Rutsche, Schütte.
6 **to recount:** nacherzählen.
7 **way away up:** weit weg droben.
to swirl: wirbeln.
dreaming (auch: *dreamtime*) (Austral.): Traumzeit, -welt (Schlüsselbegriff des mythischen Weltverständnisses der Aborigines, der der Gegenwart eine urzeitlich spirituelle Dimension verleiht).
9 **mumbling:** Gemurmel.
12 **to nestle:** sich einnisten, schmiegen.
18 f. **to catch up on the news:** sich auf dem laufenden halten.
23 **drizzle:** Niesel-, Sprühregen.

heavy black clouds soak into his soul. But he hated the rain, that day, for it was there and his little quiet wife was dead.

He just has the rain – and his tears. All his secrets and the love the half-caste girl had taught him, dripping from his puzzled eyes.

When he was alone, he became roaring drunk and smashed up his house that he and the girl had been so proud of then went and started a brawl amongst the Nyoongah people.

He might have been getting older, but his huge angry fists put three of the men in hospital. He was put in jail.

The next morning the boss came and got him out. As he walked down the muddy street in the sultry sun, everyone stared at him, shocked or disgusted at the damage he had done. He followed his boss's footsteps like a huge dog.

So he lost even his pride and gave up.

He worked at the store for a few more years. Every time he thought of his woman he went out and got drunk. He lived in a little humpy in the bush, where no one could find him.

The Community Welfare took away his children one day whilst he was out hunting. All except the baby, whom Mrs Haynes the boss's wife was looking after.

7 **roaring drunk:** maßlos betrunken.

9 **brawl:** Krakeel, Krawall.

10 **Nyoongah** (Austral.): speziell: Aborigine-Stamm des Südwestens; allg: jd., der (teilweise) von den Aborigines abstammt.

15 **sultry:** schwül.

22 **humpy** (Austral.): Eingeborenenhütte.

24 **Community Welfare:** Wohlfahrtsamt.

He never saw his children again.
He did not shear any more, as he was getting too old. Beer fat lay over him, like bird dung greening a famous statue.
Just as he had been shearing beside the white men and had gained a type of pride, now he could drink beside white men with another sort of pride. They were all brothers now – getting drunk together.
He left to wander.
He has memories of countless tin-and-asbestos towns with cold white people and whining brown people. He has memories of crowded hotels and fights, and falling asleep, drunk in the slimy gutter or under a tree. He tried his hand at boxing on a showground troupe. But soon he fell down, forever. His body was left to moulder where it lay, while the laughter bored into him like busy constant ants.

Boys drag lazily past, going nowhere. Cigarettes hang from their thin lips, phallus-like, to prove they are men.
The old man would like to beg for a smoke, but the wine he has drunk today thickens his tongue. All that comes

3 **dung:** Kot.
to green: grün färben.
10 **countless:** unzählige.
tin-and-asbestos: (aus) Blech und Asbest.
13 **slimy:** glitschig, schlammig.
gutter: Gosse.
14 **to try one's hand at s.th.:** sich an etwas versuchen.
showground troupe: Zirkus-, Kirmestruppe.
15 **to moulder:** vermodern, verschimmeln.
16 **to bore into s.o.:** sich in jdn. hineinbohren.

out of his mouth is a thin dribble of saliva that hangs off his scraggly grey beard.

Devils dance out of the boys' black eyes. They swagger, shout and laugh loudly. The words and laughter are caught by the fingers of the Moreton Bay fig trees. Later, they will be dropped to rot away with the stinking, sticky fruit. But the boys don't know that.

Two peel away from the sly dark group and squat down beside him.

"G'day, ya silly ole black bastard. Gettin' stuck into th' gabba at this time a day? Hey, ya wanna tell us 'ow ya was the state boxer, ole man?"

"Look at the metho 'e's got 'ere, Jimmy."

"Unna? 'E got no sense."

"Look out, Snowman! Featherfoot comin' your way, ya ole murderer."

"Jesus, don't 'e stink, but?"

1 **dribble:** Getröpfel.
saliva: Speichel.
2 **scraggly:** zerzaust.
3 **to swagger:** großtun; einherstolzieren.
5 **Moreton Bay fig tree:** australische Gummibaumart.
7 **sticky:** klebrig.
8 **to peel away:** ausscheren.
to squat down: sich niederhocken.
10 **G'day:** *Good day*!
ya: *you*.
ole: *old*.
to get stuck into s.th. (slang): tüchtig bei etwas zulangen.
11 **gabba:** *gabby* (Austral., slang): ‚Stoff', Alkohol.
a: *of*.
wanna: *want to*.
13 **metho** (Austral., slang): *methylated spirits* (pl.): Methylalkohol.
14 **unna** (Austral., slang): *isn't that so:* nichwahr?
17 **but** (adv., slang): absolut, total.

They laugh.

He smiles, uncomprehending, and nods his head. He knows they are laughing at him. Once he would have leaped to his feet and pulverised the whole group. That was a long time ago, though. He cannot remember.

They steal $20 from him with quick black fingers. They always do, every pension day. Where they had been afraid of his powers before, now they laugh and steal from him. He has no people to look after him. Only himself.

He sits under the tree, surrounded by empty wine bottles. He staggers over to the tap and bumps into two young girls, who shriek and squeal with mirth at him.

"The Snowman's drunk!" they shriek.

Once, they would have had to respect and admire him, as he told them about the ways and laws of their tribe.

Once.

Now they have no tribe, and he has no ways.

He half-fills a bottle with water and pours the last of his methylated spirits into it. He sits and drinks, lonely.

He watches as the groups gather in circles. People wander from one group to another or stagger across to the hotel, waiting on the corner. The tribe goes walkabout. They stumble over to the brick toilets, as lonely as he is.

4 **to pulverise:** zermalmen.
5 **though** (adv., coll.): aber, allerdings.
12 **to bump into s.o.:** jdn. anrempeln.
13 **to squeal:** quietschen.
25 **walkabout** (Austral.): (auf) Wanderschaft (Schlüsselbegriff der Aborigines für ihr territorial markiertes, aber weiträumiges Verhältnis zum Land, hier ironisch trivialisiert).

They clutch onto the tight circles and pass the drink and words around.
Drink gets hot, words get hot in the cold wind.
The boys strip off their shirts and fight out their quarrels, while the women join them or egg them on.
The people play jackpot or two-up or poker. Some grow rich, some grow poor; almost everyone grows drunk.
Everyone goes home, to wherever home is.
He stays.
The sky gets darker and more oppressive. Then it rains.
First there are the whipcracks rattling across the sky, rolling and growling like puppies playing in the fleeciness of the clouds. The lightning leaps and bounces like children; here, there and gone. The rain starts off fat and slow but becomes faster and leaner.
He just sits there, finishing off his metho and wishing he had a smoke. He suddenly vomits up all his pension day money. All over his coat and face and trousers.
Time to sleep.
The old Aboriginal lies underneath his tree that cannot

1 **to clutch onto s.th.:** sich an etwas klammern.
1 f. **to pass s.th. around:** etwas die Runde machen lassen.
5 **to egg s.o. on:** jdn. anstacheln.
6 **jackpot:** Jackpot (Poker mit steigendem Einsatz).
two-up (Austral., slang): Glücksspiel mit Münzen.
10 **oppressive:** drückend schwül.
12 **whipcrack:** Peitschenknall.
13 **puppy:** Welpe.
13 f. **fleeciness:** Vliesartigkeit (vgl. *fleecy clouds*: Schäfchenwolken).
14 **to bounce:** hüpfen.
16 **lean:** mager, dünn, fein.
18 **to vomit up:** erbrechen.
21 **Aboriginal:** (australischer) Ureinwohner.

help him, for it, too, is old and sparse of gentle green leaf. The tree and the man get wet; neither cares, though.

So cold. The rain runs in streaks down his face and body. It washes the vomit off him, with soft hands. The pattering of the rain is interrupted only occasionally by short harsh coughs.

In the early hours of the morning, the cruising police van that, like the gardener, is searching for a few weeds to pull up by the roots and throw in the bin, finds him.

His rain has taken him away from his useless, used-up life. Perhaps back to the Dreamtime he understood.

No one knew the old Wongi was dead until the next pension day.

1 **to be sparse of s.th.:** spärlich mit etwas gesegnet sein, kaum etwas haben.
5 f. **to patter:** prasseln.
8 **to cruise:** herumfahren.
police van: Polizeiwagen (zum Gefangenentransport).
10 **bin:** Abfalltonne.

Frank Moorhouse

From a Bush Log Book 1

That Christmas he went into the Budawang Ranges with his decadent friend, Belle.

They had debauched in motel rooms and restaurants along the coast while he turned forty, bed sheets drenched with champagne and with all the smells and fluids that two bodies could be made offer up in such dark love-making as, in their curious way, he and Belle were drawn into. But the conversations in the restaurants had become unproductively sadistic as they exhausted amiable conversation.

He'd gone increasingly into interior conversation with himself about "turning forty" because she was too young to have empathy with his turning forty. And he was trying to salve the loss of his young girlfriend who was overseas and "in love".

2 **log book:** Reisetagebuch.
3 **Budawang Ranges** (pl.): Bergkette innerhalb des Great Dividing Range Australiens. Diese und die folgenden geographischen Angaben beziehen sich alle auf den Osten von New South Wales, die Heimatregion des Autors.
5 **to debauch:** sich Ausschweifungen hingeben.
7 **to drench:** durchnässen.
8 **to offer up:** darbringen, aufbieten.
9 **dark** (fig.): düster, freudlos, mysteriös.
love-making: Geschlechtsverkehr.
12 **amiable:** liebenswürdig.
15 **empathy:** Einfühlung(svermögen).
16 **to salve:** beschwichtigen.

He also had some home-yearnings which came on at Christmas. His family was not in town for this Christmas, but anyhow his home-yearnings had been displaced over the years away from his family in the town to the bush about fifty kilometres away from, but behind, the coastal town where he had grown up – the Sassafras bush in the Budawang Ranges.

He'd put camping gear in the car when they'd left the city and they drove as deep into the bush as the road permitted and then left the car and backpacked their way.

As they walked deeper into the bush he kept glancing at Belle to see if she was being affected by the dull warm day and the bush. He knew the creeping hysteria and dread which the Australian bush could bring about.

She saw him looking back at her and said, "I'm coping. Stop looking back at me all the time."

They walked for an hour or so and came to what is called Mitchell Lookout.

"This is called Mitchell Lookout," he said, "but as you can see it is not a lookout in the Rotary sense."

1 **home-yearnings:** Anwandlungen von Heimweh.
to come on: aufkommen.
3 f. **to displace:** verdrängen.
7 **Sassafras:** Sassafrasbaum.
8 **camping gear:** Camping-Ausrüstung.
10 f. **to backpack one's way:** mit dem Rucksack loswandern, -ziehen (*backpack:* Rucksack).
14 **creeping:** schleichend (Krankheit).
16 **to cope:** (einer Sache) gewachsen sein.
19 **lookout:** Aussichtsstelle.
21 **Rotary:** Rotarier (Anhänger des Rotary Club, einer exklusiven internationalen Männervereinigung mit der Devise des privaten und öffentlichen »Dienens«, hier vor allem eine amerikanische Institution).

It was a shelf of rock with a limited view of the gorge.
"Lookouts are an eighteenth-century European act of nature worship which Rotary clubs have carried on. The growth is too thick – you can't see the river down there. You'll have to take my word for it."
"I can see that the growth is too thick."
"Laughably, the only thing you can see clearly from Mitchell Lookout is directly across the gorge – they could have another lookout which looked across at Mitchell Lookout."
He saw her look across at the other side and back again. She made a small movement of her mouth to show that she didn't think it was particularly "laughable".
"I don't go into the bush for views," he said.
"Tell me – what do you go into the bush for?"
"I go into the bush to be swallowed whole. I don't go into the bush to look at curious natural formations – I don't marvel at God's handiwork."
For reasons he could not explain and did not record in his log book, he decided to put the tent on the rock ledge overlooking the gorge.
"You'll find sleeping on the rock is OK," he said, "it is really much better than you imagine."
"If you say so," she said, dumping her backpack.
"I go into the bush for raw unanalysed sensory expe-

1 **shelf of rock:** Felsplatte, -vorsprung.
gorge: Schlucht.
7 **laughably** (adv.): lächerlich.
17 **natural formation:** Naturgebilde.
18 **handiwork:** Schöpfung.
20 **ledge:** (Fels-)Vorsprung, Sims.
24 **to dump:** abladen, fallen lassen.
25 **sensory:** sensorisch (die Sinne betreffend).

rience," he said, "I don't go in for naming things geologically or birds and so on."

"You don't have to apologise for not knowing the names of the birds and the stones."

He cut some bracken fern to lie on, more as a gesture towards the idea of what made for comfort.

"That'll do a fat amount of good," Belle said.

"It's a gesture."

He put up the tent, pinning each corner from inside with rocks and tying the guy ropes to rocks.

"I've even used rocks as pillows," she said.

She sat, one leg crossed over the other, cleaning dirt from her painted fingernails with a nail file.

He instantly doubted whether she had ever used a rock for a pillow and whether sleeping on rock was in fact OK.

"There," he said, "the tent is up."

She looked across at it, got up, went over and looked inside the tent but did not go in.

"How about a drink?" he said.

"Sure it's the happy hour. Any hour can be a happy hour." She laughed at this to herself.

He went about getting the drink.

"I'll cook the Christmas dinner. That'll be my contribution," she said.

"No," he said, "that's OK I'm used to cooking on camp fires."

"Look – you may be fourth-generation Australian but

5 **bracken fern:** Adlerfarn.
7 **to do a fat amount of good** (slang, iron.): herzlich wenig bringen.
10 **guy rope:** Spannseil, -schnur.
21 **happy hour:** ‚blaue Stunde', Cocktail-Stunde.
28 **fourth-generation:** seit vier Generationen.

you're not the only one who can cook on a camp fire, for godsake."

"All right, all right."

As they had their bourbons he doubted whether she could cook on camp fires. He thought about what they could salvage to eat.

"I came through the Australian experience too," she said.

"Do you know what to do if you get lost in the bush?" he asked her.

"No, I didn't mean to invite a test, but you tell me, what do I do if I get lost in the bush?"

"You stay where you are, mix a dry martini and within minutes someone will be there telling you that you're doing it wrong."

"Ha ha. Wouldn't mind a martini now this very minute."

He had never seen her cook a meal. It was always restaurants and luxury hotels, that was their relationship.

"But it was my idea to come out here in the bush – let me cook it."

"I'll cook it."

"OK – if you feel happy about it."

"I feel quite happy about it, Hemingway."

She made a low, slow fire, just right, and rested the pannikins and camp cooking dishes on the coals. It wasn't quite the way he would have done it but he didn't say anything.

1 f. **for godsake** (coll.): *for God's sake:* um Gottes willen.
6 **to salvage:** bergen, verwerten.
26 f. **pannikin:** Pfännchen.

Wood coals look stable until things tilt and spill as the wood burns away.

She squatted there at the fire. She first put potatoes on the coals. She put on the rabbit pieces – which they had not themselves hunted, he hadn't brought the guns – after smearing them with mustard and muttered to herself *"lapin moutarde"*, laughing to herself. She wrapped the rabbit in tin foil and wormed the pieces down into the coals with a flat stick. Then she crossed herself. She put the corn cobs on to boil, candied the carrots with sugar sachets from the motel, put on the beans. She then heated the lobster bisque, throwing in a dash of her bloody mary, again saying something to herself that he didn't catch.

Maybe a gypsy incantation.

She put the plum pudding on to be warmed and mixed a careful custard.

1 **stable:** stabil.
to tilt: kippen.
to spill: überschwappen.
3 **to squat:** (sich) hocken.
6 **mustard:** Senf.
7 **lapin moutarde** (Fr.): Kaninchen in Senf.
8 **tin foil:** Stanniol, Aluminiumfolie.
to worm: zwängen, bugsieren.
9 **to cross o.s.:** sich bekreuzigen.
10 **corn cob:** Maiskolben.
to candy: kandieren.
11 **sachet:** Tütchen.
12 **lobster bisque:** Hummersuppe.
dash: ‚Schuß', Spritzer.
13 **bloody mary:** Cocktail aus Wodka und Tomatensaft.
15 **gypsy:** Zigeuner(in).
incantation: Beschwörung, Zauberformel.
17 **custard:** Vanillesauce.

She squatted there at the smoking fire, stirring and moving the pots as needed, throwing on a piece of wood at the back at the right time for some quick heat, all with what he thought was primitive control. He swigged bourbon from a First World War officer's flask and passed it to her from time to time. He liked to think that the flask had belonged to one of his great-grandmother's lovers. She squatted there in silence, full of attention for what she was doing.

He swigged the bourbon and, from time to time, became a First World War officer. She had slipped into a posture which belonged to the primitive way of doing things – what? – a few thousand years ago when the race cooked on camp fires. Or more recently, back to Settlement.

He sat off on a rock and took some bearings using his Swiss compass and Department of Mapping 1:25 000 topographic maps, trying to identify some of the distant peaks.

"Shrouded God's Mountain," he said.

"Good," she said, not looking up.

He kept glancing at her, enjoying her postures.

He opened a bottle of 1968 Coonawarra Cabernet Shiraz.

4 **to swig:** hastig trinken, ‚kippen'.
5 **flask:** Feldflasche.
13 **race:** Menschengeschlecht.
14 f. (*First*) **Settlement:** (Erst-)Besiedlung Australiens durch die Briten (1788).
16 **to take bearings:** den Standort bestimmen, sich orientieren (*bearings* [pl.]: Kompaßkurs).
17 **Department of Mapping:** Vermessungsamt.
20 **to shroud:** einhüllen.
23 f. **Coonawara Cabernet Shiraz:** australischer Rotwein.

"It's ready," she said, muttering something.

She presented the meal with perfect timing, everything right, at the right time, no over-cooking, no cold food, no ash or grit in the food. She served it on the disposable plates they'd bought.

He complimented her.

"Don't sound so surprised," she said.

They ate their Christmas dinner and drank the wine in the Guzzini goblets he'd bought for camping, and as they did, a white mist filled the gorge and stopped short of where they were so that they were atop of it, as if looking out the window of an aircraft above the clouds.

It came almost level with the slab where they were camped and were eating.

"Jesus, that's nice," he said, staring down at the mist.

"I thought you didn't go in for God's handiwork."

"Well I don't go searching for it. When he does it before my very eyes, I can be appreciative."

She looked down at the mist while chewing the meat off a rabbit bone, as if assessing the mist, aesthetically? theologically? She ate the meal with her fingers, with their painted nails.

2 **timing:** zeitliche Abstimmung.
3 **to over-cook:** verkochen.
4 **grit:** Grus.
4 f. **disposable plate:** Party-, Einwegteller.
9 **goblet:** Becher.
11 **to be atop of s.th.:** (oben) auf etwas sein.
14 **slab:** (Fels-)Platte.
17 **to go in for s.th.:** für etwas zu haben sein, etwas für eine Sache übrig haben.
19 **appreciative:** empfänglich.
21 **to assess:** würdigen.

"It's all right," she said, emphatically.

It was warm and there were bush flies which worried her and she kept brushing them away with her hand, cursing at them.

"Piss off you bastards," she said.

"I've made peace with the flies," he said. "Sooner or later in the Australian bush you have to stop shooing the flies and let them be."

"I'm not going to let them be," she said, "I'm going to give them a bad time."

"Please yourself."

"I will."

"You did the meal perfectly."

"Thank you – but you aren't the only person in Australia who can cook on a camp fire." She then laughed, and said, "Actually it was the first time I have cooked a meal on a camp fire."

"It was perfect. You looked very primitive – you could have been out of the First Settlement."

"I felt very primitive," she said, "if the truth be known."

"I meant it in the best sense."

"I assumed you did."

They sat there with food-stained hands, smoky from the fire, food and wine on their breath. Belle exposed her legs to the misty sun.

She stared expressionlessly at him, her hand methodi-

2 **bush fly:** australische Fliegenart.
3 **to brush:** (mit der Hand) abwehren.
5 **Piss off you bastards** (slang): Haut ab, ihr Scheißkerle!
7 **to shoo:** verscheuchen.
10 **to give s.o. a bad time:** jdm. das Leben schwer machen.
20 f. **if the truth be known:** wenn du's wissen willst, genaugenommen.

cally waving away the flies, and she then began to remove her clothing. They had sex there on the rock slab surrounded by the mist. They played with the idea of her naked body on the rock slab, the bruising of it, the abrasion. He held her head by the hair and pinned her arms, allowing the flies to crawl over her face. She struggled but could not make enough movement to keep them off her face. She came and he came.

They drank and became drowsy watching, from a cool distance, the fire burning away.

During the night he got up because he liked to leave the tent in the dead of the night and prowl about naked. He said to himself that although he did not always feel easy in the bush, in fact, he sometimes felt discordant in it, he'd rather be out in it feeling discordant than not be there.

"What are you doing out there for godsake?" Belle called from the tent.

"Having a piss."

He crawled back into the tent.

"I thought for a moment you were communing," she said.

"Just checking the boundaries."

4 **to bruise:** quetschen, prellen.
5 **abrasion:** Abschürfung, Schramme.
8 **to come** (coll.): ‚kommen', einen Orgasmus haben.
9 **drowsy:** schläfrig.
12 **in the dead of:** mitten in.
to prowl about: herumstreichen, -schleichen.
14 **discordant:** unharmonisch, uneins.
19 **to have a piss** (vulg.): pinkeln, schiffen.
21 **to commune:** (spirituell) kommunizieren.
23 **to check the boundaries** (pl.): das Terrain markieren, Gelände abstekken.

In the morning he said, "Well, it wasn't unsleepable on the rock."

"No, not unsleepable," she said, and smiled, "not unfuckable either."

"The rock tells our body things our mind cannot comprehend."

"Don't give me that bullshit."

It was still misty and the air heavy with moisture but it was not cold.

Neither of them now wanted to stay longer in the bush although they'd talked initially of staying "for a few days".

He thought he might have stayed on if he'd been alone.

They struck camp.

"I liked having if off on the rock," she said, "I seem to be bruised."

"But you were bruised enough?" he ritualistically asked, resolving that he would not make that joke again because of its tiredness, resisting what the tiredness meant about their relationship.

"Hah, hah."

It was a grey sky. The dampness quietened everything down just a little more than usual and the dull sky dulled everything a little more, including their mood.

7 **Don't give me that bullshit** (vulg.): Komm mir nicht mit so 'nem Scheißdreck!
11 **initially** (adv.): anfangs.
15 **to strike camp:** das Lager abbrechen.
16 **to have it off** (slang): es treiben (Sex).
18 **ritualistically** (adv.): ritualistisch, das Ritual befolgend.
20 **tiredness:** Lahmheit.

They hoisted on their backpacks and began walking.
"I know all about abjection and self-esteem but for a slut like me it's all a game now."
He gestured to indicate that he wasn't making judgements about it.
"It's no longer the whole damned basis of my personality," she said.
"You have to be a bit like that to go into the bush anyhow. It's very easy to make it self-punishing."
"I was thinking that."
They walked a few metres apart. They passed a stand of grey kangaroos some way off which speculatively watched them walk by. Belle and he indicated to each other by a glance that they'd seen the kangaroos.
"More of God's handiwork," she called.
He realised as they walked out that he had a disquiet about being there with Belle. When he looked at the Christmas they'd just had together – on paper – it was untroubled, memorable, an enriched event – the mist in the gorge, the perfect camp-fire meal, the good wine. Belle naked on the rock, his standing on the ledge in the dead of night, the melancholy bush.
The disquiet came because Belle had been moved *out of place* in his life. The Budawang bush was the place of his childhood testing, his family's bush experience,

1 **to hoist:** hochhieven.
2 **abjection:** Niedergeschlagenheit.
self-esteem: Selbstachtung.
3 **slut:** Nutte.
11 **stand:** (Stand-)Platz.
12 **speculatively** (adv.): grüblerisch, sinnierend.
23 f. **to move out of place:** an die falsche Stelle rücken.
25 **testing:** Erprobung, Prüfung.

touching base, touching primitive base. He had learned his masculinity here.

She did not belong in that album.

He looked back at her up the trail, plodding through the swampy part in her Keds dripping wet from the moisture of the bushes. He saw her again at the camp fire, primitively squatting. He felt a huge fondness for her.

They'd often said that they were not the sort of person either would really choose to spend Christmas or birthdays with, they were making do with each other.

By bringing Belle with him on his fortieth birthday and on Christmas he had left an ineradicable and inappropriate memory trace across the countryside.

But she was also somehow an embodiment of his great-grandmother, they'd divined that in Katoomba at his great-grandmother's grave. But this was not his great-grandmother's territory.

He was then struck by a splintering observation – the Budawangs and the Blue Mountains of Katoomba were part of the Great Dividing Range but in his head they were different mountains, different districts. His great-grandmother and Belle belonged at Katoomba, the

1 **to touch base:** das Mal erreichen (Baseball); hier (fig.): auf die natürliche Basis des Menschen zurückkommen.
2 **masculinity:** Männlichkeit.
4 **to plod:** sich dahinschleppen, stapfen.
5 **swampy:** sumpfig, morastig.
Keds: amerikanisches Schuhfabrikat.
10 **to make do:** Vorlieb nehmen.
12 **ineradicable:** unausrottbar.
13 **memory trace:** Erinnerungsspur.
14 **embodiment:** Verkörperung.
15 **to divine:** ahnen.
18 **to splinter:** sich aufsplittern.

decayed health resort and spa. It was there that his great-grandmother had used her charms and beauty to make her living, her fortune. The Budawangs were where he'd been the boy scout and the army officer. The parts still didn't quite come together.
He caught up with Belle and touched her fondly.
"Sorry about the mud," he said.
"I can cope. I can take it."
This was where he'd learned as a boy how to "take it".
"I'll get you a new pair of Keds."
"They come from the States."
"I'll get a pair sent across."
"You probably won't."

In a motel on the coast they showered off the mud, dried off the dampness, turned up the air-conditioner to warm and got slowly drunk, sprawled on the floor. Belle with a towel wrapped around her drying hair, in a silk kimono, was like a cat back in habitat.
He spread out the map of southern New South Wales. These are my heartlands, he showed her, the English damp green tablelands of Bowral and Moss Vale, the old goldfields, the lakes of Jindabyne, the new snow resort, down to Bega where my father introduced me to the

1 **health resort:** Kurort.
spa: Badeort.
6 **to catch up with s.o.:** jdn. einholen.
14 **to shower off:** abbrausen, -duschen.
16 **to sprawl:** ausgestreckt daliegen, sich rekeln.
18 **habitat:** Standort, Zuhause.
20 **heartland:** Herz-, Kernland.
21 **tableland:** Tafelland.
22 **snow resort:** Winterurlaubsort.

man who had a library of a thousand books of mystery and the supernatural, to Kiama where my girlfriend from school and I went for our miserable honeymoon after we married in the hometown Church of England.

And Milton, where I found ten years of *Champion* magazine in an old newsagency.

He told her how he had been a rebellious but highly proficient scout, had played football up and down the coast, had been a soldier on manoeuvres there, had surfed the whole coast, camped out and hunted in all the bush.

"You're a very sentimental person," she said, as she rubbed cream into a scratch on her leg.

"No, I don't think I am."

"I think you are."

"I think not."

"A sentimental drunk, then."

"There is another territory."

He circled the Katoomba and Jenolan Caves district.

"My great-grandmother's territory."

"We've done that."

"And there is my grandfather's territory." He circled the town. "He committed suicide in the hotel there. But that

1 f. **books of mystery and the supernatural:** Kriminalromane und phantastische Geschichten.

4 **hometown:** heimatstädtisch, örtlich.

4 f. **Church of England:** Anglikanische Kirche.

6 **"Champion":** britische Jungen-Zeitschrift (während der fünfziger Jahre populär in Australien).

9 **proficient:** geübt, bewandert.

11 **to camp out:** im Freien zelten.

24 **to commit suicide:** Selbstmord begehen.

was not his territory, maybe being what he was he had no territory."

But neither were ever mentioned in this territory, he told her, pointing at the first heartlands circle.

Belle was leaning on his shoulder pretending an interest, for an instant she became someone else leaning on his shoulder looking at the map, a high-spirited late arrival at a dying party.

"Let's go," he said, "let's check out now and go back to the city. I think it's over."

Two weeks later he went back to the Budawangs and camped again in the same place, alone. It was a trip to erase the mistake of having gone there with Belle.

He realised, as he sat there in the bush at Mitchell Lookout, that it was a misguided effort. Coming back to erase it had only more deeply inscribed it.

Now whenever he passed the place he would think of having gone there with the wrong person, of having taken his great-grandmother into the hard country where she didn't belong. He would laugh about Belle, squatting there cooking, about the flies on her face, and Belle saying, "I feel quite happy about it, Hemingway."

7 **high-spirited:** ausgelassen, aufgekratzt.
8 **dying:** zu Ende gehend.
9 **to check out:** das Hotel (nach Begleichung der Rechnung) verlassen.
13 **to erase:** tilgen.
15 **misguided:** irregeleitet, verfehlt.
16 **to inscribe:** eingravieren, einmeißeln.

Helen Garner

What We Say

I was kneeling at the open door, with the cloth in my right hand and the glass shelf balanced on the palm of my left. She came past at a fast clip, wearing my black shoes and pretending I wasn't there. I spoke sharply to her, from my supplicant's posture.

"Death to mother. Death," she replied, and clapped the gate to behind her.

It had once been a kind of family joke, but I lost the knack of the shelf for a moment and though it didn't break there was quite a bit of blood. After I had cleaned up and put the apron in a bucket to soak, I went to the phone and began to make arrangements.

In Sydney my friend, the old-fashioned sort of friend who works on your visit and wants you to be happy, gave me two tickets to the morning dress rehearsal of *Rigoletto*. I went with Natalie. She knew how to get there and which door to go in. "At your age, you've never been inside the *Opera* House?" Great things and

5 **at a fast clip:** im Eiltempo.
7 **supplicant:** (unterwürfiger) Bittsteller.
posture: Körperhaltung.
8 f. **to clap to:** zuschlagen.
10 f. **to lose the knack of s.th.:** den kniffl ichen Halt von etwas verlieren.
17 **dress rehearsal:** Generalprobe.
18 **"Rigoletto":** 1851 uraufgeführte Oper von Giuseppe Verdi (1813 bis 1901).

small forged through the blinding water. We hurried, we ran.

At thc first interval we went outside. A man I knew said, "I like your shirt. What would you call that colour – hyacinth?" At the second interval we stayed in our seats so we could keep up our conversation which is no more I suppose than exalted gossip but which seems, because of her oblique perceptions, a most delicate, hilarious and ephemeral tissue of mind.

At lunchtime we dashed, puffy-eyed and red-cheeked, into the kitchen of my thoughtful friend. He was standing at the stove, looking up at us over his shoulder and smiling: he likes to teach me things, he likes to see me learning.

"How was it?"

"Fabulous! We cried *buckets*!"

Another man was leaning against the window frame with his arms crossed and his hair standing on end. His skin was pale, as if he had crept out from some burrow where he had lain for a long time in a cramped and twisted position.

1 **to forge:** vorankommen, vorstoßen.
3 **interval:** (Theater-)Pause.
7 **exalted:** gehoben; begeistert.
8 **oblique:** indirekt, verquer.
hilarious: ausgelassen, übermütig.
9 **ephemeral:** flüchtig.
tissue: (fig.) (feines) Gewebe.
10 **puffy-eyed:** mit geschwollenen Augen.
16 **fabulous:** fabelhaft, phantastisch.
to cry buckets (coll.): etwa: Stein und Bein heulen.
18 **to stand on end:** zu Berge stehen.
19 **burrow:** Erdloch, Höhle, Unterschlupf.
20 **cramped:** verkrampft.

"You cried?" he said. "You mean you actually shed tears?"

Look out, I thought; one of these. I was still having to blow my nose, and was ready to ride rough-shod. My friend put the spaghetti on the table and we all sat down.

"I'm starving," said Natalie.

"What a plot," I raved. "So tight you couldn't stick a pin in it."

"What was your worst moment?" said Natalie.

"Oh, when he bends over the sack to gloat, and then from off-stage comes the Duke's voice, singing his song. The way he freezes, in that bent-over posture, over the sack."

The sack, in a sack. I had a best friend once, my intellectual companion of ten years, on paper from land to land and then in person: she was the one who first told me the story of *Rigoletto* and I will never forget the way her voice sank to a thread of horror: "And the murderer gives him his dauther's body on the river bank, *in a sack*." A river flows: that is its nature. Its sluggish water can work any discarded object loose from the bank

4 **to ride rough-shod** (fig.): rücksichtslos vorgehen, schurigeln (*rough-shod:* roh beschlagen [Pferd]).
8 **to rave:** schwärmen, sich begeistern.
tight: straff (Handlung).
11 **to gloat:** sich weiden, frohlocken.
12 **off-stage:** hinter der Bühne.
19 **thread:** hier: Unterton.
21 **sluggish:** träge (fließend).
22 **to work loose:** lockern, losmachen.
to discard: ablegen, ausrangieren.

and carry it further, lump it lengthwise, nudge it and roll it and shift it, bear it away and along and out of sight.

"Yes, that was bad, all right," said Natalie, "but mine was when he realized that his daughter was in the bedchamber with the Duke."

We picked up our forks and began to eat. The back door opened on to a narrow concrete yard, but light was bouncing down the grey walls and the air was warm, and as I ate I thought, Why don't I live here? In the sun?

"Also," I said, "I *love* what it's about. About the impossibility of shielding your children from the evil of the world."

There was a pause.

"Well, yes, it is about that," said my tactful friend, "but it's also about the greatest fear men have. Which is the fear of losing their daughters. Of losing them to younger men. Into the world of sex."

We sat at the table quietly eating. Words which people use and pretend to understand floated in silence and bumped among our heads: virgin; treasure; perfect; clean; my darling; anima; soul.

Natalie spoke in her light, courteous voice. "If that's what it's about," she said, "what do you think the

1 **to lump:** (mit anderem) zusammenwerfen.
lengthwise: der Länge nach.
to nudge: stupsen.
5 f. **bedchamber:** Schlafgemach.
8 **concrete:** Beton.
9 **to bounce:** prallen, schnellen.
12 **to shield s.o. from s.th.:** jdn. vor etwas beschirmen.
21 **to bump:** purzeln, rumpeln.
22 **anima** (Lat.): 1. Seele (Philosophie); 2. Seelenbild der Frau im Unbewußten des Mannes (Psychologie).

women in the audience were responding to?" – for in our bags were two sodden handkerchiefs.

The salad went round.

"I don't know," said my friend. "You tell me."

We said nothing. We looked into our plates.

"That fear men have," said my friend. "Literature and art are full of it."

My skin gave a mutinous prickle. *Your* literature.

"*Do* women have a fundamental fear?" said my friend.

Natalie and I glanced at each other and back to the tabletop.

"A fear of violation, maybe?" he said. He got up and filled the kettle. The silence was not a silence but a quietness of thinking. I knew what Natalie was thinking. She was wishing the conversation had not taken this particular turn. I was wishing the same thing. Stumped, struck dumb: failed again, failed to think and talk in that pattern they use. I had nothing to say. Nothing came to my mind that had any bearing on the matter.

Should I say "But violation is our destiny"? Or should I say "*Nothing can be sole or whole / That has not been rent*"? But before I could open my mouth, a worst moment came to me: the letter arrives from my best

2 **sodden:** durchnäßt.
8 **mutinous:** aufrührerisch.
prickle: Prickeln, Kribbeln.
13 **violation:** Schändung, Vergewaltigung.
17 **to stump** (coll.): verblüffen, ratlos machen.
18 **to strike dumb:** sprachlos machen.
20 **to have any bearing on s.th.:** in irgendeinem Zusammenhang mit etwas stehen.
22 f. **"Nothing can be sole ... rent":** W. B. Yeats, »Crazy Jane Talks with the Bishop«, Z. 17 f. (*to rend:* zerreißen).

friend on the road in a far country: "He was wearing mirror sun-glasses which he did not take off, I tried to plead but I could not speak his language, he tore out handfuls of my hair, he kicked me and pushed me out of the car, I crawled to the river, I could smell the water, it was dirty but I washed myself, a farm girl found me, her family is looking after me, I think I will be all right, please answer, above all, don't tell my father, love." I got down on my elbows in the yard and put my face into the dirt, I wept, I groaned. That night I went as usual to the lesson. *All I can do is try to make something perfect for you, for your poor body, with my clumsy and ignorant one:* I breathed and moved as the teacher showed us, and she came past me in the class and touched me on the head and said, "This must mean a lot to you – you are doing it so beautifully."

"Violation," said Natalie, as if to gain time.

"It would be necessary," I said, "to examine all of women's writing, to see if the fear of violation is the major theme of it."

"Some feminist theoretician somewhere has probably already done it," said the stranger who had been surprised that *Rigoletto* could draw tears.

"Barbara Baynton, for instance," said my friend. "Have you read that story of hers called *The Chosen Vessel*? The woman knows the man is outside waiting for dark.

1 **on the road:** unterwegs, auf Reisen.
2 **mirror sun-glasses** (pl.): Sonnenbrille mit Spiegelgläsern.
12 **clumsy:** unbeholfen.
21 **theoretician:** Theoretiker(in).
24 **Baynton:** Barbara B. (1857–1929), australische Schriftstellerin.
25 **"The Chosen Vessel":** Kurzgeschichte in Barbara Bayntons *Bush Studies* (1902).

She puts the brooch on the table. It's the only valuable thing she owns. She puts it there as an offering – to appease him. She wants to buy him off."

The brooch. The mirror sunglasses. The feeble lock. The weakened wall that gives. What stops these conversations is shame, and grief.

"We don't have a tradition in the way you blokes do," I said.

Everybody laughed, with relief.

"There must be a line of women's writing," said Natalie, "running from the beginning till now."

"It's a shadow tradition," I said. "It's there, but nobody knows what it is."

"We've been trained in *your* tradition," said Natalie. "We're honorary men."

She was not looking at me, nor I at her.

The coffee was ready, and we drank it. Natalie went to pick up her children from school. My friend put in the plug and began to wash the dishes. The stranger tilted his chair back against the wall, and I leaned on the bench.

"What happened to your hand?" he said.

"I cut it on the glass shelf yesterday," I said, "when I was defrosting the fridge."

1 **brooch:** Brosche.
2 **offering:** Opfer(gabe).
2 f. **to appease:** besänftigen, beschwichtigen.
3 **to buy s.o. off:** jdn. abfinden.
5 **to give:** nachgeben.
7 **bloke** (coll.): Kerl.
15 **honorary:** Ehren-.
19 **plug:** Stöpsel.
to tilt: kippen.
24 **to defrost:** (Kühlschrank) abtauen.

"There's a packet of Bandaids in the fruit bowl," said my friend from the sink.

I stripped off the old plaster and took a fresh one from the dish. But before I could yank its little ripcord and pull it out of its wrapper, the stranger got up from his chair, walked all the way round the table and across the room, and stopped in front of me. He took the Bandaid and said,

"Do you want me to put it on for you?"

I drew a breath to say *what we say*: "Oh, it's all right, thanks – I can do it myself."

But instead, I don't know why, I let out my independent breath, and took another. I gave him my hand.

"Do you like dressing wounds?" I said, in a smart tone to cover my surprise.

He did not answer this, but spread out my palm and had a good look at the cut. It was deep and precise, like a freshly dug trench, bloody still at the bottom, but with nasty white soggy edges where the plaster had prevented the skin from drying.

"You've made a mess of yourself, haven't you," he said.

1 **Bandaid:** Markenname für ein Heftpflaster.
3 **plaster:** (Wund-)Pflaster.
4 **to yank:** losreißen.
ripcord: Reißfaden.
5 **wrapper:** Hülle.
10 **to draw breath:** Atem, Luft holen.
15 **to dress:** (Wunde) verbinden.
19 **trench:** Graben.
20 **nasty:** garstig.
soggy: feucht.
22 **to make a mess of o.s.:** (iron.) sich ganz schön zurichten.

"Oh, it's nothing much," I said airily. "It only hurt while it was actually happening."

He was not listening. He was concentrating on the thing. His fingers were pale, square and clean. He peeled off the two protective flaps and laid the sticky bandage across the cut. He pressed one side of it, and then the other, against my skin, smoothed them flat with his thumbs, and let go.

1 **airily** (adv.): leichthin.
4 **to peel off:** abstreifen, lösen.
5 **protective flap:** Schutzlasche.
sticky: klebrig.

Editorische Notiz

Das Glossar erklärt in der Regel alle Wörter, die über die Wertigkeitsstufe 4 des *Englischen Arbeitswörterbuches* von Alfred Haase (Frankfurt a. M.: Moritz Diesterweg [7]1979) hinausgehen. Im Zweifelsfall wurde großzügig verfahren, d. h. eher eine Vokabel mehr aufgenommen als dort vorgesehen. Die einzelnen Texte sind unabhängig voneinander glossiert.

Im Glossar verwendete Abkürzungen

adv.	adverb
arch.	archaic (veraltet)
Austral.	Australian
coll.	colloquial (umgangssprachlich)
fig.	figuratively (übertragen)
Fr.	French
Lat.	Latin
iron.	ironical
Norw.	Norwegian
o.s.	oneself
pl.	plural
s.o.	someone
s.th.	something
vulg.	vulgar (vulgär, derb)

Textnachweise

Murray Bail: The Drover's Wife. In: M. B.: Contemporary Portraits and Other Stories. St. Lucia: University of Queensland Press, 1975. S. 55–61. – Copyright © Murray Bail 1975.

Peter Carey: American Dreams. In: P. C.: The Fat Man in History. London: Faber and Faber, 1980. S. 147–157. – Copyright © University of Queensland Press, St. Lucia, Queensland 1974, © Peter Carey 1979.

Helen Garner: What We Say. In: Murray Bail (Hrsg.): The Faber Book of Contemporary Australian Short Stories. London: Faber and Faber, 1988. S. 300–304. Erstdruck in »The Sydney Morning Herald«, 6. Januar 1987. – Copyright © Helen Garner. Mit Genehmigung der Agentur Barbara Mobbs, Edgecliff (N. S. W.).

David Malouf: The Only Speaker of His Tongue. In: D. M.: Antipodes. London: Chatto & Windus, 1985. S. 68–72. – Copyright © David Malouf 1985. Mit Genehmigung von Random Century Group, London.

Frank Moorhouse: From a Bush Log Book 1. In: F. M.: Forty-Seventeen. Ringwood (Vict.): Viking, 1988. S. 23 bis 31. – Copyright © Frank Moorhouse 1988. Mit Genehmigung von Penguin Books Australia Ltd., Ringwood (Vict.).

Archie Weller: Pension Day. In: A. W.: Going Home. Sydney: Allen & Unwin, 1986. S. 68–73. – Copyright © Archie Weller 1986. Mit Genehmigung von Allen & Unwin Australia Pty. Ltd., Sydney.

Patrick White: Down at the Dump. In: P. W.: The Burnt Ones. London: Eyre and Spottiswoode, 1964. S. 283–314. – Copyright © Patrick White 1964. Mit Genehmigung der Agentur Barbara Mobbs, Edgecliff (N. S. W.).

Fay Zwicky: Hostages. In: F. Z.: Hostages. Fremantle (W. A.): Fremantle Arts Centre Press, 1983. S. 1–6. Copyright © Fay Zwicky 1983.

Literaturhinweise

I. Allgemeine Darstellungen

Arens, Werner, »The Ironical Fate of ›The Drover's Wife‹: Four Versions from Henry Lawson (1892) to Barbara Jefferis (1980)«, in: *The Story Must Be Told: Short Narrative Prose in the New English Literatures*, hrsg. von Peter O. Stummer, Würzburg: Königshausen und Neumann, 1986, S. 119–133.

Bennett, Bruce, *Australian Short Fiction: A History*, St. Lucia: University of Queensland Press, 2002.

Bennett, Bruce / Strauss, Jennifer (Hrsg.), *The Oxford Literary History of Australia*, Melbourne: Oxford University Press, 1999.

Gelder, Ken / Salzman, Paul, *The New Diversity: Australian Fiction 1970–88*, Melbourne: Longman Cheshire, 1989.

Goldsworthy, Kerryn, »Short Fiction«, in: *The Penguin New Literary History of Australia*, hrsg. von Laurie Hergenhan, Ringwood (Vict.): Penguin, 1988, S. 535–546.

Jose, Nicholas, »Possibilities of Love in Recent Australian Stories«, in: *The Story Must Be Told: Short Narrative Prose in the New English Literatures*, hrsg. von Peter O. Stummer, Würzburg: Königshausen und Neumann, 1986, S. 134–143.

Maack, Annegret, »Die Auseinandersetzung mit amerikanischen Einflüssen in der australischen *short story*«, in: *Literatur in Wissenschaft und Unterricht* 17 (1984) S. 339–351.

Ross, Bruce Clunies, »Some Developments in Short Fiction, 1969–1980«, in: *Australian Literary Studies* 10, Heft 2 (1981) S. 165–180.

Torre, Stephen, *The Australien Short Story, 1940–1980: A Bibliography*, Sydney: Hale and Iremonger, 1984.

Webby, Elizabeth, »Australian Short Fiction from *While the Billy Boils* to *The Everlasting Secret Family*«, in: *Australian Literary Studies* 10, Heft 2 (1981) S. 147–164.

Wilde, W. H. [u. a.]. *The Oxford Companion to Australian Literature*, Melbourne: Oxford University Press, 1985.

Wilding, Michael, »The Tabloid Story Story« (1978), in: *Days of Wine and Rage*, hrsg. von Frank Moorhouse, Ringwood (Vict.): Penguin, 1980, S. 145–154.

II. Studien zu einzelnen Autoren und ihrer Kurzprosa

Bindella, Maria Teresa, »Crossing Boundaries in David Malouf's *Antipodes*«, in: *Quaderni di Lingue e Letterature* 19 (1994) S. 109–123.

Burrows, J. F., »The Short Stories of Patrick White«, in: *Ten Essays on Patrick White*, hrsg. von G. A. Wilkes, Sydney: Angus and Robertson, 1970, S. 163–181.

Craven, Peter, »Murray Bail: The Homemade Modernist Finds a Heart«, in: *Heat* 8 (1998) S. 75–91.

Gilbert, Pam, »Helen Garner«, in: P. G., *Coming Out from Under: Contemporary Australian Women Writers*, London: Pandora, 1989, S. 5–24.

Goldsworthy, Kerryn, *Helen Garner*, Melbourne: Oxford University Press, 1997.

Hassall, Graham, *Dancing on Hot Macadam: Peter Carey's Fiction*, St. Lucia: University of Queensland Press, [3]1998.

Heltay, Hilary, »Nachwort«, in: Patrick White, *Down at the Dump / Drunten auf der Müllkippe*, übers. von H. H., hrsg. von Walter Pache, Stuttgart: Reclam, 1975, S. 83–103.

Indyk, Ivor, *David Malouf*, Melbourne: Oxford University Press, 1993.

Little, Janine, »›Deadly‹ Work: Reading the Short Fiction of Archie Weller«, in: *Australian Literary Studies* 16, Heft 2, (1993) S. 190–199.

Myers, David, *The Peacocks and the Bourgeoisie: Ironic Vision in Patrick White's Shorter Prose Fiction*, Adelaide: Adelaide University Union Press, 1978.

Pons, Xavier, »Weird Tales: Peter Carey's Short Stories«, in:

Telling Stories: Postcolonial Short Fiction in English, hrsg. von Jacqueline Bardolph, Amsterdam: Rodopi, 2001, S. 391–407.

Raines, Gay, »The Short Story Cycles of Frank Moorhouse«, in: *Australian Literary Studies* 14, Heft 4 (1990) S. 525–435.

Sharrad, Paul. »A Delicate Business: David Malouf's Shorter Prose«, in: *World Literature Today* 74, Heft 4 (2000) S. 759–768.

Tiffin, Chris, »Relentless Realism: Archie Weller's *Going Home*«, in: *Kunapipi* 10, Heft 1–2 (1988) S. 222–235.

Turner, Graeme, »American Dreaming: The Fictions of Peter Carey«, in: *Australian Literary Studies* 12, Heft 4 (1986) S. 431–441.

Woodcock, Bruce, *Peter Carey*, Manchester: Manchester University Press, 1997.

Zwicky, Fay, »Writing in the Eighties«, in: *Westerly* 3 (Oktober 1984) S. 59–64. [Interview mit David Kerr.]

Nachwort

Zur Entwicklung der australischen Kurzgeschichte

Die zeitgenössische australische Kurzgeschichte kann auf die – für eine der neueren englischsprachigen Literaturen – beachtliche Tradition von einem Jahrhundert zurückblicken. Entstanden ist sie im Zuge der Bemühungen einheimischer Autoren um ein vom Kolonialerbe sich lösendes Nationalbewußtsein und eine entsprechend eigenständige Literatur. Der entscheidende Entwicklungsschub ging von Erzählern wie Henry Lawson und Barbara Baynton aus, die sich in den neunziger Jahren des 19. Jahrhunderts um die führende Zeitschrift *The Bulletin* geschart hatten und mit ihren Kurzgeschichten prototypische Texte schufen, die weit über die eigene Schaffenszeit und teilweise über die Gattungsgrenzen hinaus traditionsbildend sein sollten. Zu den Wesensmerkmalen dieser Literatur gehört die Konzentration auf das weiträumige Hinterland (»outback«) als mythisierte Schauplatzdomäne charakteristisch australischen Lebens und den entsprechenden Heldentypen des Busch-Pioniers, der sich beherzt gegenüber seiner widrigen Umwelt zu behaupten weiß und im männlich-kameradschaftlichen Kodex der »mateship« Rückhalt findet. Das bevorzugte literarische Verfahren war ein auf Objektivität zielender sozialer Realismus, der die geradlinig verknappte Erzählweise im zurückhaltend einfachen bis umgangssprachlichen Stil pflegte. In der australischen Kurzgeschichte dominierten diese Grundzüge trotz mancher Abwandlungen bis zur Mitte des 20. Jahrhunderts.

Erst in den sechziger Jahren zeichneten sich deutliche Verschiebungen einer thematischen und formalen Erneuerung ab. Hier ist neben Hal Porter vor allem Patrick White zu nennen, der das repräsentativere Australien der zeitgenössischen Vorstädte ins Blickfeld rückte und die Leere des menschlichen Innenlebens mit psychologischer Subtilität und stilistischer Komplexität ironisierte. Solche Vorstöße eines der literarischen Moderne verpflichteten Autors bereiteten eine Gegenbewegung vor, die Anfang der siebziger Jahre die Gattung in mancher Hinsicht revolutionär veränderte. Initiiert wurde diese neue Welle durch Frank Moorhouse und Michael Wilding, deren Magazin *Tabloid Story* (seit 1972) das Programm einer alternativen Kurzgeschichtenpoetik vorstellte. Statt der bodenständigen »bush tales« mit ihrer Figuren- und Situationsstereotypik, realistischen Eindimensionalität und geschlossenen Struktur forderte man die Öffnung zur internationalen (vor allem amerikanischen) Postmoderne des phantastisch ausgreifenden Fabulierens, des parodistischen Spiels, der Grenzverwischung von Realität und Fiktion, der prozessualen Selbstreflexivität und keinen Zusammenhang erzwingenden fragmentarischen Form, wie auch der spontanen Bekenntnishaftigkeit und unvoreingenommenen Wandlungsbereitschaft, die sich in der freizügigen Thematisierung von Tabus (zumal der Sexualität) und dem radikalen politischen Engagement (etwa für diskriminierte Minderheiten) ausdrückte.[1] In solchen Postulaten schlägt sich zugleich der liberale, explorative Zeitgeist der – von den USA ausgegangenen – kosmopolitischen Counter Culture nieder. In Australien stellte diese Gegenbewegung die tradierten Vorstellungen von der nationalen Identität wieder gründlich in Frage. Zu den Ambivalenzen der Entwicklung gehört, daß die Kritik an der fortschreitenden Amerikanisierung Australiens als einer Art Neokolonialismus auch die Gegenargumente weitgehend aus dem Ursprungsland dieser Kultur bezog.

Für die australische Literatur hatte nicht zuletzt die Lockerung der Zensur in dieser Dekade eine befreiende Wirkung, selbst wo sie in den Konventionen des Realismus verdrängte Lebensbereiche erschließen wollte. Im übrigen ging es auch experimentierfreudigeren Erzählern wie Moorhouse, Peter

1 Vgl. Michael Wilding, »The Tabloid Story Story« (1978), in: *Days of Wine and Rage*, hrsg. von Frank Moorhouse, Ringwood (Vict.): Penguin, 1980, S. 145–154.

Carey und Murray Bail nicht ausschließlich um eine Ablösung des überkommenen Realismus, sondern vorrangig um eine pluralistische Auffächerung der Literatur – ganz abgesehen von der Tatsache, daß sie in der erzählerischen Praxis oft genug – und gerade in einigen ihrer besten Texte – hinter den formulierten Theorien zurückblieben. Die große Mehrheit der zeitgenössischen Kurzprosaautoren schreibt ohnehin durchaus realistische Geschichten. Nur handelt es sich im Gefolge der Gattungserneuerung auf breiter Basis um einen wesentlich differenzierteren Realismus, der sich durch psychologische Subtilität, anspielungsreiche Suggestivität, ironische Mehrdeutigkeit und erzählerische wie sprachliche Komplexität als eine sehr viel flexibler gewordene Darstellungsweise auszeichnet.

Zu den Neuerungen der Gegenwartsliteratur, von denen auch die Kurzprosa profitiert, gehört außerdem das wachsende Bewußtsein einer Gesellschaft überwiegend anglo-keltischen Ursprungs für die Probleme ethnischer Minderheiten und einer Kultur dominant männlicher Leitbilder für die Belange der Frauen. Beides spiegelt sich in der Aktualität bestimmter Autor(inn)en und deren Gruppierungen wider. Immigranten, Aborigines und Frauen finden zunehmend ihre Stimme in einer Zeit, da Australien verstärkt nicht-nordeuropäische Einwanderer aufgenommen hat, mit großer Verspätung den Ureinwohnern ihre Bürgerrechte zugestanden hat und im Zuge des internationalen Feminismus den Frauen mehr Gleichberechtigung einräumt. Die Kurzgeschichten von Fay Zwicky, Archie Weller und Helen Garner können dazu beitragen, daß das Selbstverständnis der Australier sich im Sinne des multikulturellen Miteinanders und der Neudefinition des Geschlechterverhältnisses verändert. Viele Autoren – nicht nur der Minderheitengruppen – haben zudem eine meist autobiographisch motivierte enge Bindung an begrenzte heimische Regionen, so daß auch im kulturgeographisch differenzierten Sinne Australien erst jetzt von der Literatur systematisch erschlossen wird.

Zu den vorliegenden Kurzgeschichten

»Down at the Dump« (1963) ist die bekannteste Kurzgeschichte von Patrick White (1912–91), des großen alten Mannes der neueren australischen Literatur. Der Text entwickelt in komprimierter Form viele seiner typischen Motive und Methoden. Symptomatisch sind die Dualismen, die seine höchst ambivalente Einstellung zu Australien zum Ausdruck bringen. Der Autor, der sich lange als Fremder im eigenen Land empfinden mußte, zeigt hier einen satirischen Ausschnitt jenes tristen Sydneyer Vorstadtlebens, das sich weithin im Konformismus eines materialistischen Spießbürgertums über die innere Leere hinwegtäuscht, während die wenigen, die imaginative Sensibilität und emotionale Intensität beweisen, als Außenseiter erscheinen. Die Konstellation der Figuren und Gruppen veranschaulicht entsprechende Gegensätze von Leben und Tod, Liebe und Haß, Schein und Sein. Um den Todesfall von Daise, die über ihr Leben hinaus die Botschaft der – erotischen wie karitativen – Liebe verkündet, scharen sich mit ihren charakteristischen Reaktionen die Hogbens, die als lebendig Tote den oberflächlichen Durchschnitt vertreten, und die Whalleys, die in ihrer Sinnenfreude zwar Vitalität bezeugen, aber letztlich doch auch ein reduziertes Leben führen und Randständige bleiben; sodann die beiden Jugendlichen, die sich einander annähern und nicht nur die Kluft zwischen ihren beiden Familien überwinden können, sondern auch einen durch Daise inspirierten eigenen Weg finden mögen. Daise ist die kontroverse Orientierungsfigur, die sich im Affront gegen ihr gutbürgerliches Herkunftsmilieu mit einem geistig zurückgebliebenen Tramp einläßt und in ihrer elementaren Offenheit, Warmherzigkeit und Einfühlsamkeit alternative Maßstäbe setzt. White unterstützt das komplementäre Erzählkonzept mit Hilfe symbolischer Schauplätze (vor allem Friedhof und Müllkippe, benachbarte Ruhestätten und Orte der Liebesoffenbarung) und einer an filmische Kompositionsmethoden erinnernden Technik der Reihung kurzer, durch Schnitt- und Überblendungseffekte markierter

Szenen mit permanentem Perspektivwechsel. Die vorherrschende Thematik wird so immer wieder neu variiert.
Trotz der Verlegung des Schauplatzes in ein Provinznest berührt sich »American Dreams« (1974) mit Whites Geschichte, da auch hier eine materialistisch eingestellte und verlogen agierende Gesellschaft bloßgestellt wird. PETER CAREY (geb. 1943) gehört allerdings zu einer anderen Erzählergeneration, die sich gegenüber der von White vertretenen Moderne eher den Prinzipien der Postmoderne zugewandt hat. Carey versteht es besonders, australischer Alltagsrealität auf beklemmende Weise phantastische Züge zu verleihen. Die Parabel des rätselhaften Vermächtnisses eines Einzelgängers, der ein die Mitbürger typisierendes Miniaturmodell des Heimatortes anfertigt, demonstriert einmal die ambivalenten Amerikanisierungsträume, die in der Nachkriegszeit bis ins australische Hinterland vorgedrungen sind, aber im Falle der Verwirklichung – hier der touristischen Vermarktung des Modells als einer Art Disneyland – die Erwartungen der meisten enttäuschen. Der Text versinnbildlicht zugleich metaliterarisch die Komplikationen eines künstlerischen Vermittlungsversuchs. Der Modellbauer schafft als »verrückter« Außenseiter ein herausfordernd getreues Abbild seiner Kleinstadt, das die Mitbürger in der Überschaubarkeit und Detailliertheit fasziniert, aber durch die Einblicke hinter die Fassaden auch irritiert und schließlich ein dumpfes Unbehagen hinterläßt. Während das einheimische Publikum je nach persönlicher Betroffenheit das Modell kontrovers interpretiert, sind die amerikanischen Besucher so auf die Übereinstimmung von Konterfei und Original fixiert, daß sie den Porträtierten keine Weiterentwicklung zugestehen wollen. Die dramatisierte Konstellation von Anschauungsobjekt und Betrachterstandpunkten wird ironisch in ihren Widersprüchen belassen, einschließlich des nur beschränkt urteilsfähigen Ich-Erzählers. Der Paradoxie der Entwicklung sind alle ausgeliefert: Die erträumte Realität erscheint als Opfer der realen Fiktion. Zugleich zerstört der das Individuum anziehende amerikanische Traum, indem er zerbricht und den Ort

entzweit, den stärker gemeinschaftsgebundenen australischen Traum. Carey unterstreicht durch den systematischen Einsatz von Verfremdungseffekten solche Verschiebungen und Verkehrungen, wenn er das Abnorme in die Normalität eindringen läßt, das Geschehen mit Bildern des Todes und der Leere unterminiert und die dialektische Symbolik des ein- bzw. ausgrenzenden Mauerbaus oder des zwanghaften Schauens ohne Einsichtsfähigkeit entwickelt.

Wie in Careys Geschichte geht es auch in »The Drover's Wife« (1975) von Murray Bail (geb. 1941) um die Konfusion des Interpreten, der ein Abbild im Hinblick auf seine Vorlage in einem charakteristisch australischen Kontext betrachtet. Der Erzähler, der auf einem Gemälde seine verschwundene Frau wiederzuerkennen glaubt und sich in assoziativen Mutmaßungen über ihr Schicksal und in apologetischen Erinnerungen an ihre Ehe ergeht, verwechselt Realität (Malermodell) und Fiktion (Bildfigur) und bekundet eine Kunstauffassung, die weniger das Werk erhellt als den Betrachter enthüllt. Mit spielerischer Ironie benutzt Bail den naiven Erzähler vor allem aber auch zu einer multimedialen, intertextuellen Revision eines in den Künsten verbreiteten Nationalmythos. Denn bei dem Gemälde handelt es sich um das tatsächliche Bild »The Drover's Wife« (1945) von Russell Drysdale, der wiederum eine gleichnamige Kurzgeschichte (1892) von Henry Lawson illustriert. Lawsons archetypischer Text porträtiert die Pioniersfrau im Busch, die sich – auch ohne ihren Mann – im täglichen Daseinskampf bewährt und die Kinder vor einer Schlange beschützt. Drysdale bestätigt mit der standhaften Überlebensgröße der Frau und der abweisenden Öde der Landschaft diese Grundzüge, deren Stereotypik von Bail aber unterminiert wird. In satirisch-parodistischen Verdrehungen gibt er die Allgemeinverbindlichkeit des Mythos den subjektiven Obsessionen des Erzählers preis, verlegt er den Ausgangspunkt des Geschehens in das gegenwartsnahe städtische Kleinbürgermilieu und entwirft er gegensätzliche Ansichten von Busch und Viehtreiber: Was für den Erzähler befremdliche Ausflugsimpressionen sind, regeneriert die in der urbanen Öde verkümmerte Ursprünglichkeit der Frau, wofür der verlassene Mann verständnislos nur ihre »verrückten Anwandlungen« verantwortlich machen kann. Bails Geschichte ist die erste einer Reihe ähnlicher Alternativversionen des Sujets, die in einer Kettenreaktion von zeitgenössischen Kurzgeschichtenautoren wie Frank Moorhouse, Barbara Jefferis und Anne Gambling verfaßt worden sind.[2]

FAY ZWICKY (geb. 1933) behandelt in der Titelgeschichte ihrer Sammlung *Hostages* (1984) das wiederkehrende Thema der Jugendlichen, die gegen die gutbürgerliche Ordentlichkeit und zumal die Bevormundung durch die Mutter rebelliert und dabei einen schmerzvollen Lernprozeß durchmacht, und sie verknüpft dies mit dem Problem des leidgeprüften Emigrantenschicksals, um zweierlei Opfer unmenschlicher Unterdrückung in der Melbourner Vorstadt zusammenzubringen: die vor der Nazi-Verfolgung in der fremdländischen Ferne Zuflucht suchende alleinstehende Jüdin und das vereinsamte, komplexbeladene Mädchen aus einer fest etablierten jüdischen Einwandererfamilie. Während die Mutter aus gruppensolidarischer Pflicht die Emigrantin als Klavierlehrerin beschäftigt, macht die Tochter den Eindringling zum Sündenbock ihrer aufgestauten Aggressivität, die diese erst recht in die Rolle der Außenseiterin drängt und systematisch vertreibt. Erst spät gelangt die Heldin zu der verstörenden Einsicht, daß sie beide »Geiseln« sind, existentiell bedrohte Einzelwesen in einer übermächtigen Umwelt, die sie – bewußt oder unbewußt, physisch oder psychisch – zu vernichten trachtet. Die konfliktreiche Identitätssuche der Tochter mit

2 Moorhouse benutzt die Vorlagen in »The Drover's Wife« (1980; Nachdr. in: F. M., *Room Service*, Ringwood [Vict.]: Penguin, 1985, S. 98–116) zu einer übermütig anzüglichen Interpretationsparodie. Jefferis kontert in »The Drover's Wife« (in: *The Bulletin*, 23./30. Dezember 1980, S. 156 bis 160) mit einer feministischen Umperspektivierung. Gambling bietet in »The Drover's DeFacto« (in: *Latitudes: New Writings from the North*, hrsg. von Susan Johnson und Mary Roberts, St. Lucia: Queensland University Press, 1986, S. 149–159) die aktualisierte Version der Gefährtin eines »trucker drover«.

ihrer kompensatorischen Abreaktion führt zum alptraumhaften Gewahrwerden einer Schicksalsgemeinschaft mit der – nun zweifach – vertriebenen Frau: Auch unter der Oberfläche des australischen Lebens lauern erschreckende menschliche Abgründe, wenngleich deren Ausmaß nicht mit dem Grauen des Holocaust vergleichbar ist.
Deutet sich bei Zwicky das Problem des grenzüberschreitenden Kulturkonflikts in den Kommunikationsschwierigkeiten von australischem Teenager und deutscher Emigrantin an, so rückt es in der Kurzgeschichtensammlung *Antipodes* (1985) von DAVID MALOUF (geb. 1934) variationsreich ins Zentrum. Das Antipoden-Bewußtsein Australiens am »anderen« Ende der Welt, das zum charakteristischen Themenrepertoire der australischen Literatur gehört, wird von Malouf in den Polaritäten zwischen Australiern und Europäern – als Reisenden in der Ferne, entwurzelten Einwanderern, randständigen Exilanten oder gewandelten Heimkehrern – veranschaulicht und über die Gegensätze zwischen der Alten und Neuen Welt hinaus mit elementaren Dualismen wie Leben und Tod, Kontinuität und Wandel oder Sprache und Schweigen verbunden. In »The Only Speaker of His Tongue« zeigt Malouf dies an der Begegnung eines norwegischen Forschungsreisenden mit einem Aborigine, der als letzter Überlebender seines Stammes gilt und eine zum Aussterben verurteilte Sprache spricht. Die Konfrontation der beiden Außenseiter auf australischem Boden wird aus der Sicht des passionierten Sprachwissenschaftlers wiedergegeben, der die einmalige Chance, etwas über die archaische Sprache und deren andersartiges Weltbild zu erfahren und festzuhalten, nicht wahrnimmt, da er sich scheut, in der kolonialistisch vorbelasteten Fremdsprache Englisch in ihn einzudringen und ihn zum kulturanthropologischen Objekt zu degradieren. Die Situation verdeutlicht den tragischen Untergang einer gedankenlos ausgerotteten bodenständigen mündlichen Kulturtradition, deren letzter Zeuge – von seinem ursprünglichen Lebensraum abgeschnitten – sie nur noch in seinem Kopf bewahrt: Der Rest ist Schweigen. Eine Ironie besteht darin, daß

der Weiße von weit her kommen muß, um die Tragweite des Verlusts zu erfassen. Als Lexikograph, der – mit seiner Muttersprache in der Ferne isoliert – zutiefst verunsichert wird, kann er allein sich in die Situation des Aborigine hineinversetzen.

Aus der Sicht des unmittelbar Betroffenen führt der Aborigine-Autor ARCHIE WELLER (geb. 1958) in seiner Kurzgeschichtensammlung mit dem ironischen Titel *Going Home* (1986) die in der Misere der randständig verstädterten Aborigines verkommene Ureinwohnerkultur vor Augen. Wie in »Pension Day« demonstriert er häufig die vorübergehende Illusion des Erfolgs und der Anerkennung des Aborigines in der Welt der Weißen, die in der unentrinnbaren Erfahrung der Entwurzelung und Diskriminierung zerbricht, so daß trotz desperater Rückbezüge auf die angestammte Kultur und eines stoischen Überlebenswillens das Schicksal jedes einzelnen in Alkohol, Gefängnis oder Tod endet. Die Geschichte exemplifiziert den Werdegang eines Aborigines in Westaustralien vor und nach der – für ihn unerheblichen – bürgerrechtlichen Anerkennung (1967), der aus seinem autochthonen Lebensraum (den naturreligiösen und sozialen Bindungen ans heimische Territorium und der eigengesetzlichen Gemeinschaft von Familie und Stamm) herausgerissen wird und in der Außenwelt der Weißen und Mischlinge ein neues Leben beginnen muß, das nach einer relativ glücklichen Zeit als meisterhafter Schafscherer und Wiederverheirateter den unaufhaltsamen Niedergang ins Abseits des wohlfahrtsabhängigen trunksüchtigen Stadtstreichers bringt. Als Spottfigur der ethnisch verwandten Gassenjungen endet er – das leibhaftige Symbol eines gewaltsamen Identitäts- und Traditionsverlustes.

Gehört Weller zu den erst neuerdings hervortretenden Aborigine-Autoren, so FRANK MOORHOUSE (geb. 1938) zu den maßgeblichen Erneuerern der Kurzprosa der frühen siebziger Jahre, und er hat sich ausschließlicher als die meisten seiner Zeitgenossen der Weiterentwicklung dieser Gattung gewidmet. Er tut dies allerdings hauptsächlich in

»clusters of stories«, die sich zu buchlangen Zyklen zusammenfügen und das andere von ihm vertretene Prinzip des »discontinuous narrative« (ob inhaltlich sprunghaft oder formal fragmentarisch) durch Querbezüge ausbalancieren. Dies wird bei »From a Bush Log Book 1« schon dadurch besonders deutlich, daß die Beschreibung des Busch-Trips mit der Freundin komplementär einen weiteren Bericht über eine Einzeltour des Erzählers nach sich zieht, der den mißratenen Versuch, den Fehlschlag der ersten Reise wettzumachen, wiedergibt. Es geht dabei vor allem um die satirisch-parodistische Ironisierung des zeittypischen Bedürfnisses der kosmopolitischen Intellektuellen »to touch base«.[3] Der Versuch, sich einer urtümlichen Lebensgrundlage wieder zu vergewissern, offenbart nicht zuletzt modische Attitüden und kompensatorische Zwänge. Der Erzähler wird von einer Midlifecrisis umgetrieben, die jugendliche Freundin spielt die Rolle der dekadenten Dirne, und beide nehmen im aktuellen Lebensstil von Camping und Counter Culture die Posen einer Naturnähe ein, die doch nichts an der gewohnten Raffinesse eines erotischen, kulinarischen Hedonismus vermissen läßt. Der Erzähler kann die regionalen »Wurzeln« seiner Kindheit nur mehr auf der Karte studieren, und so sehr er den Mißerfolg des Naturtrips der Deplaciertheit der Freundin im Hinterland anlasten möchte, wird deutlich, daß auch er seinen Ursprüngen entfremdet ist. Vermittelt wird die Reiseerfahrung im typisch lakonischen, auch selbstironischen Stil, der im Gefolge des amerikanischen New Journalism zur pointenhaft verknappten Formulierung und Aneinanderreihung von Momentaufnahmen sowie bizarren Details tendiert und zugleich eine Parodie der traditionsreichen australischen *explorer*-Tagebücher liefert.

Helen Garner (geb. 1942) rückt ähnlich wie Zwicky in ihrem Erzählwerk vorzugsweise Jugendliche und Frauen des Melbourner Vorstadtmilieus mit ihren charakteristischen Konflikten ins Zentrum, aber sie bringt stärker die Sehweisen

3 Vgl. F. Moorhouse, »The Bush Against the Laundromat«, in: *Days of Wine and Rage*, hrsg. von F. M., S. 391–401.

einer Generation ein, die unter dem Einfluß feministischer Ideen aufgewachsen ist. In »What We Say« (1988) verkörpert die Ich-Erzählerin – zusammen mit ihrer kosmopolitischen Freundin – die Frau mit einem kritischen Emanzipationsbewußtsein, die sich gleichwohl gegenüber der renitenten Tochter wie dem souverän auftretenden Sydneyer Freund und dessen Bekannten in der Alltagspraxis verwundbar zeigt. Dies wird nicht nur durch das Rahmenmotiv ihrer Handverletzung versinnbildlicht und durch ihr resignatives Eingehen auf die Rolle der männlichen Beistand brauchenden schwachen Frau dramatisiert, sondern ist durchgängig gegenwärtig im Themenkomplex der Frauenbedrohung durch sexuelle Gewalttätigkeit: Die melodramatische, doch nahegehende Handlung von Verdis *Rigoletto* anläßlich eines Opernbesuchs, das Trauma der besten Freundin als Vergewaltigungsopfer in der fernen Fremde, das einheimische Sujet des Sexualmords in Barbara Bayntons »The Chosen Vessel« zeigen dies nachdrücklich an. In einer männerdominierten Gesellschaft wie der australischen mit ihrer eigenen Sexismustradition (»mateship«) stellt sich das Problem der Artikulierbarkeit frauenrechtlicher Ansprüche mit besonderer Dringlichkeit. Jedenfalls schafft die Erzählerin es nicht, sich selbst in ihrem relativ liberalen Umkreis aus den Zwängen der bevormundenden Männerwelt zu befreien. Ihre Proteste bleiben stumm, da sie keine Stimme findet, die zwischen den unterschiedlichen Sprachen von Männern und Frauen vermitteln könnte – dies ist wohl auch der Sinn des lakonischen Titels, der auf die Doppeldeutigkeit der ernstgemeinten Entgegnung (»Was wir hingegen behaupten«) und der halbherzigen Äußerung (»Was wir so sagen, ohne es wirklich zu meinen«) abhebt. Wie die Geschlechter haben auch andere minderheitliche oder mehrheitliche Gruppen innerhalb der australischen Gesellschaft ihre divergierenden Lesarten der Welt und Sprechweisen ihrer Vermittlung entwickelt, die pluralistisch zu umreißen eine der vordringlichen Funktionen der zeitgenössischen australischen Kurzgeschichte ist.

Eberhard Kreutzer

Inhalt

Patrick White
Down at the Dump 3

Peter Carey
American Dreams 60

Murray Bail
The Drover's Wife 80

Fay Zwicky
Hostages 90

David Malouf
The Only Speaker of His Tongue . . 101

Archie Weller
Pension Day 109

Frank Moorhouse
From a Bush Log Book 1 122

Helen Garner
What We Say 138

Editorische Notiz 147

Textnachweise 149

Literaturhinweise 151

Nachwort 155